Unlovely Child

By Marsha T. Cowan

Unlovely Child
(a song)

I understand how father God could treat me so unkind,
It's hard to love an unlovely child,
But easy to bend his mind.

When walls of youth come tumbling down, the heart
comes crashing, too,
And all that's left is an empty life,
And a soul that's torn in two.

Oh, won't you leave your palace bright and mend my
walls with me,
And find my spirit from among the stones,
And set my wounded soul free...

Set my wounded soul free!

Chapter One

It was brisk that morning with sparkling streams of sunlight seeping into her bedroom window through the kitchen towels that were hung as curtains. Nine-year-old Lydia blinked her eyes a few times and tried to remember why she was sleeping in the bedroom off the back porch--the one reserved for hired help--but nothing would register in her sleepy brain, so she rose and sat on the edge of the old ticking mattress, propping her tan spindly legs on the edge of the wire mesh springs by the back of her heals, and tried harder to remember. A clicking sound came to her ears. Looking up, Lydia saw Duke, her white, curly haired companion, tiptoeing across the bare wooden floor to where she was sitting. He put his front paws on her knees and leaned forward to lick her face.

Suddenly, she felt soreness on her legs where her dog was putting his weight, and as he licked her face, she could feel it stinging. Lydia pushed Duke aside and, wincing with each step, went to get the little piece of mirror that lay on the side table on the screened back porch of the old Victorian farm house. Looking into it earnestly, she could see many scratches on her face and neck along with bruises around her throat.

Gasping, she squinted to get a closer look and then, remembering the discomfort in her legs, began to pull up her dress-- why was she still wearing her dress?--to examine the soreness. On her legs and stomach there were more scratches and bruises. Lydia began to whimper. What had happened to her? Why was she in the back porch bedroom alone all night? Terror seized her heart, and for a moment, she was frozen, unable to breathe. A crashing noise in the bedroom off the kitchen entrance startled her and broke her panic enough to move.

Earl was standing in front of the whitewashed fireplace holding a slender bottle of cheap whiskey in one hand and leaning against the carved wooden mantle with the other: his blue uniform work shirt half tucked into his belt, his hair in disarray, his shoes untied. Abruptly, he stepped back and threw the bottle against the back bricks of the unlit fire pit. Fragments of glass went spewing out across the wooden floor, some flying through the front of his trousers, but he did not seem affected by the cutting of the glass on his shins. Shaking, Earl turned around and spotted Lydia standing wide-eyed in the doorway.

"Daddy! What're ya' doin'?" she cried and began to walk slowly and carefully into the room towards him.

"It's all yer fault, ya' know," he spit the words out like venom, glaring at her with a strange twist in his eyebrows like he was not completely sure that his words were true.

"What?" she felt sick in her stomach.

"Ya' coulda' stayed at the swing set. Ya' coulda' done what you was told, but no, ya' had to go wanderin' off with that mutt of yourn. Darius told ya' to stay where you was. He's ya' olda' brotha', and you're s'posed to do what he says when yer mom and me ain't around. You know that!"

Earl was clinching his fists by his side, trembling with passion, and Lydia was waiting for the unthinkable to happen, but he had never hit her before, so she stood her ground believing that perhaps he would not hit her now, even as he advanced slowly toward her. At that moment, eleven-year-old Darius walked into the room and stood in front of his father.

"Dad? Are you okay? It's time to go…" Darius swallowed, looking around at the broken glass, and then he saw Lydia. "Ya' ain't even dressed yet! Man! Do I have to do everythin' for ya' now?" He reached and grabbed Lydia's hand, hastily dragging her through the back porch, out the screen door, and down the rickety wooden steps to get some water.

All the water came from a well in the side yard about fifty feet from the back steps. Around two hundred years earlier, a hole had been dug about a 100 feet deep and three feet in diameter, and over the years a little box-like housing had been built around it with a hinged opening at the top through which a bucket tied to a rope could be dropped. Long before Lydia's family had rented the house, two tall 2x4 wooden braces had been attached on opposite sides with another 2x4 crossbeam connecting them making a place to attach a pulley through which ran the rope. Now one could drop the bucket through the opening, let it hit the water and fill up, and then more easily pull the heavy bucket to the top of the well. Earl had nailed a low handle to the housing and pulled the rope through it so it was low enough for Darius and Lydia to draw water. The well house box was chin height to Lydia, but Darius could reach the lid to open it and drop in the bucket.

Even with all the pulleys and handles, drawing water was still no easy task, and Darius grunted as he heaved the full bucket from over the black hole to the wide ledge of the well house. He reached for the slender handled gourd that hung on a nail on the 2x4 brace and dipped some water for Lydia to drink and then poured some more water into a metal wash pan on the ledge of the cement footing around the bottom of the well house.

"Here. At least wash yer face and hands. Ya' don't have time to change yer dress." Darius frowned down at Lydia and propped his hands on his hips. "I don't even know why I'm doin' this for ya' after all the trouble you've caused. I do know this--you had better stay the hell away from Dad if ya' want to keep breathin'."

"But why?" she whined. "What have I done? I hurt, Darius. Why's Daddy so mad at me? I thought he was gonna' hit me back there."

"How can ya' ask me that? Mama's gone now 'cause of ya', and we don't know when she'll be back, or if she'll ever come back, but for yer sake, ya'd better pray that she does. Maybe he should've hit ya', but shut up now. He's comin'."

Earl had tucked in his shirt, tied his shoes, and combed his hair. He lumbered out to the well house like a man without a spirit and studied the ground as he walked as if he might find some useful words laying in the scarce grass that grew under the mighty oaks in the side yard. When he reached the well, he looked at Darius and then at Lydia. He spoke, and his voice quivered.

"We ain't neva' goin' to talk about this no more. Eva'. Ya' hear? I don't want you kids to think about it no more. What's done is done, and we can't go back and change it. Ya' understand?"

Both children shook their heads up and down dutifully, but Lydia wanted to cry out and run to her father and be held in his strong arms and know that everything was alright.

"Since yer mama ain't here right now, Lydia, you'll have to take ova' her chores, and that means that you, Darius, will have to do both ya'll's chores by yerself. I'm goin' to work now. Git yourselves up the road to the bus stop, and don't be late," Earl turned and moved mechanically towards his old truck without saying or waving goodbye.

"Thanks loads, Lydia. Now I hafta' do twice the chores!"

"Well I hafta' do all Mama's stuff, and, and I don't even know how," she wailed uncontrollably, shaking in all her skinny bruised limbs.

Darius took her by the hand, and they began the quarter mile walk to the top of the dirt road that was their drive to catch the yellow bus to school. They had eaten no breakfast that morning, nor did they have lunch bags to take with them. Earl passed the children slowly in his truck, looking blankly at Lydia as he passed by. That would be the last time her daddy would look at her for many years. To Lydia, it just did not seem right that the sun was shining so brightly.

Earl was oblivious that morning to the lovely, playful ribbons of sunlight streaming through the trees and dancing across the dirt road, gliding unharmed over the rusty surface of his old truck, highlighting the remnants of mint green paint which was its heritage. His mind was accustomed to feeling numb as it was his habit, on his way to work, to breakfast on whiskey taken from a small bottle he kept hidden under the seat where, hopefully, Chappell would never find it. This morning, however, his anesthetized brain was the result of shock and disbelief. The sudden and unexpected events that had happened to his family had left him completely defenseless and bewildered. Chappell fully blamed him for the unspeakable tragedy, but Earl's conscience could not accept that level of guilt and responsibility. If only Lydia had stayed at the swing set with her brother! If only she had listened! None of this would have happened. Everybody would still be happy and together. What if he had never invited Mr. Woodall into their lives? The last question abruptly intruded into Earl's thoughts and his heart seemed to leap into his throat.

Earl clutched his chest as he gasped for air and then bashed the steering wheel with his fists, finally drawing in a deep breath and unleashing a horrible, tormented scream. Pulling over to the side of the road, he wept and shook for a long time until his rage subsided, then reached for his bottle under the seat, but is was not there. It was lying in glistening sharp slivers on the wooden floor of his bedroom. Earl crumpled. Sighing deeply, he wiped his nose on his shirt sleeve and then shifted his old truck into first gear. As he pulled back onto the gravel road, his besieged brain swung into survival mode, focusing on the technicalities of driving, while his spirit crept deep into the belly of his soul. Earl felt less than a man and even less a father. Perhaps if he stayed to himself, he could endure the pain of Chappell's absence, but Lydia would be a constant reminder, and no matter how hard he tried, he could not bring himself to forgive her and embrace her right now. In his eyes she was a blight on the scenery of his life that should include Chappell, but because of Lydia, Chappell was not there. He grew angrier as he thought about it until, by the time he got out of his truck at work, his teeth were clenched and his handsome countenance had turned to stone. He would show her. Lydia would pay for what she had done until the day Chappell returned--if she returned. Lydia would pay.

Poor Darius was ten pounds thinner from three months of double chores and Lydia's cooking. He began each day, before sunup, by chopping, stacking, and hauling armloads of firewood to the back porch from the covered shed behind the house, enough to last a day for cooking and heating. Lydia usually gathered all the wood chips to use for kindling in the black wood cook stove in the kitchen, but since Chappell had left, Lydia had no time for that, so even this tedious chore was now the responsibility of Darius.

After hauling wood and chips to the house, he would take four white porcelain buckets, which held three gallons each, out to the well, fill them up, and bring them back to the long table on the back porch to be used for drinking, bathing, and cooking. It took two trips now without Lydia's help. If he was lucky, Lydia would have his breakfast ready by the time he filled the buckets. If not, he would have to continue his morning chores on an empty stomach. Milking the cow was next, and the milk would be stored in the ice box until Lydia could churn it after school.

"Lydia! My breakfast ready yet?" he yelled from the back porch.

Lydia was holding onto a huge 12 inch black cast iron frying pan with both hands using a large folded hand towel for a mitt because she had accidentally burned up her mother's other two mitts long ago. She managed to land the large pan onto the table where she emptied the few eggs and bacon onto her brother and father's plates. She then heaved the heavy, hot pan back onto the stove, being sure this time to place it on the edge where the surface was cooler and where the left over grease was less likely to catch on fire. The smell of overly toasted bread reached her nostrils about the same time that her father walked into the room. He stopped, frowned, shook his head, and then sat down at his place at the end of the table.

"When ya' gonna' learn how to take the bread outa' the oven before ya' go fixin' the plates?" he scowled, mashing his eggs with the back of his fork.

Lydia stood there a second just to see if he would look up at her so she could smile at him, but he had not had any eye contact with her since that morning three months ago when her life had changed so mysteriously—was it really only three months? That is not to say that he had not had words with her. He was quick to criticize and scold her for the mistakes she made trying to do a grown woman's job with the body of a nine year old little girl. He minced no hurting words whenever the opportunity presented itself. At first Lydia had wept with each cutting remark, but gradually she learned how to shield her heart from the painful encounters by pretending that it did not matter and by throwing herself numbly into her impossible workload. After all, if the family's dilemma was entirely her fault, she had no choice but to try to make up for it to

Earl and Darius. Often she missed school because vegetables had to be canned, or clothes had to be washed which took an entire day with the old ringer washer, or she had cut herself so badly using the sharp butcher knife that her father did not want her going to school bleeding. People might notice, he'd say. Her life had become a nightmare, and at the ripe old age of nine, Lydia could no longer see a reason for living.

"Well?" Darius asked as he stepped into the kitchen. "Oh, man, finally!" He took off his hat and sat down to eat his breakfast with his father. He had to eat in a hurry, though, because the chickens still had to be fed and the hogs still had to be slopped with the left over food from yesterday mixed in a bucket with water, all of which he would do after he scoffed down his food.

Lydia sat on a straw-bottomed, ladder-backed chair at the small cupboard in the nook beside the wood cook stove trying to finish some homework from the last time she had missed school while snapping green beans from the garden into bite sized pieces and dropping them into a bowl in her lap. She could hardly keep her eyes open. Sleep was a luxury of which she rarely ever got more than five or six hours at a time, hardly enough for a fourth grader to survive. Her memory was not as quick as she was accustomed, and her mind stayed fuzzy so that trying to figure out math problems, which used to be fun to her, was now an unhappy chore. Her teacher preferred scolding her in front of the class or sitting her in the corner with a tall white dunce cap on her head, to taking her aside to ask her about her life, perhaps finding a way to help Lydia to be her old self again. Lydia's fingers were raw from scrubbing clothes, peeling vegetables, mending, and washing dishes. There were burns here and there up and down her arms where she had learned from trial and error how to make a lasting fire in the old wood cook stove and in the other wood heaters in the house. Making beds, sweeping, picking up, washing windows, cooking, canning, laundry, and sewing--all things her mother should be there doing; all things that took away from her life as a normal child.

Lydia began to harbor bitterness towards her mother for which she felt horribly guilty at times, but what was worse was the growing hatred she felt towards her father for his unjust treatment of her—or was it unjust? She could deaden her mind against his poisonous remarks and keep functioning, but she could not justify his attitude towards her and instinctively felt that it was his own sin he was trying to shift onto her, and Lydia was not convinced that she deserved it. What had she done? No one would talk about it. Was it really her fault? Was she really the reason their family had gone from normal and happy to dysfunctional and miserable? Deep inside, she could not believe that she had that kind of power, though it was of no consequence. She was imprisoned in her father's belief that she was at fault, and that was all that mattered.

Lydia put her books in her bag, got lunch bags for her brother and herself, closed all the dampers to the old wood cook stove so the fire would die down to useful embers, and started toward the back door to meet her brother who by this time had finished his chores. She grabbed his book bag from the top of the wood box on the porch and handed it to him as he walked up.

"Let's do it," he said, and off they went up the quarter mile drive to catch the yellow bus to school. As they walked up the dirt road, Darius looked at his poor exhausted little sister and gently tousled the top of her hair. He had mixed feelings about her and all that had happened, and especially its impact on all of their lives. He missed his mother terribly, and he was uncomfortable around his father and wished things could be like they used to be. Nevertheless, Darius could see that Lydia was the most buffeted by the incident, and he could not help but feel a little sorry for her, just a little sorry.

"Hey! What's the big idea?" Lydia reached up and smoothed her hair, looking down at the ground, grinning with delight that her brother had noticed her again. A tear ran down her cheek. She brushed it away before Darius could see it, and then squinted up at the bright sun, still not understanding its purpose in such a dreary life.

Darius and Lydia were expected to be honor students in school. They were given no other choice. Of course, it was not hard to be the best students in their school. Both Earl and Chappell, though of low income backgrounds, were highly intelligent and capable people, endowed with many talents. Darius and Lydia had inherited much intelligence and talent from their parents. However, over the past few months, the children had been burdened by fatigue and sadness which made it hard to concentrate and produce on the level at which they were accustomed to performing.

Darius grew angry over his plummeting grades and was often up until late at night trying to do extra work to raise them. The unfairness of this stung his heart, and he did not know who to hate the most: his mother for leaving them so suddenly, or Lydia for causing such a dilemma that his mother felt she had to leave. It never occurred to Darius--probably because he did not know the minutiae of what had transpired--to accuse Earl for the present family situation. In Darius's eyes, his father was a victim, too, so ultimately, Darius focused his bitterness on poor Lydia, and he would struggle to keep from wanting to shake her skinny limbs with all his might and yell, "Why?" at her haggard face. At those times, overwhelming grief and guilt would wash over his spirit, and young Darius would sob inconsolably, waking up the next morning face down over his notebook, the papers he had labored over blurred and smeared with tears and fit only to be thrown into the fire of the wood stove which he would solemnly do, and afterward, he would vow to guard his heart from these abysmal thoughts and try to be nicer to Lydia.

Chapter Two

Chappell was looking down at the contents of the small square white box in her hands. She was sitting in the wide stark white hallway of the hospital waiting for her afternoon session with Dr. Winthrop, her primary psychiatrist. Everything, it seemed to her, was white and bare in this place, even this little box, and so the pastel colors of the contents of the box stood out in happy soft contrast to the white sterile cotton on which it laid. It was a set of jewelry--bracelet and earrings--made from inch long natural colored squares of wood on which were glued small one-half inch square pieces of pastel tinted ceramic tiles. She had made it herself in the workshop, in an activity designed to relieve stress before sessions. Chappell had chosen aqua blue tiles and pale yellow tiles to mix together on her jewelry. At the time she was excited to be making this delightful, frivolous project, but now she was ashamed that in her possession was a constant, absurd reminder of her weakness, and of her husband's frailty. It was ironic that something so delicate and pastel and pretty could represent something else so heartbreaking and infuriating.

As she turned to put the box down beside her on the beautiful oak pew, Chappell saw Dr. Turner opening the screen door at the end of the wide hallway, his silhouette momentarily blocking the brightness of the morning light. He strolled easily over to the heavy oak pew and sat down beside Chappell, smiling sweetly at her, keeping a few feet between them. She could feel her face growing crimson under his gaze and hated herself for it. She was a married woman--a mother--and had no right to these feelings.

"So," he began, looking down at the floor, "you're going home in a couple of days, right?"

"Yeah," she said softly.

They sat in silence for a few moments. Chappell noticed, for the first time, the rhythmic ticking of the grandfather clock at the other end of the hallway. She also noticed, not for the first time, the auburn highlights in Dr. Turner's hair.

"Hey," Dr. Turner said, reaching for her small square white box, "you finished, I see. May I?" he asked, holding the box out to her.

"I don't know. It's really nothin' to look at..." she began, but he was already lifting the lid.

"I helped you pick out these tiles, remember, so how can it be nothing to look at? My taste is impeccable," He smiled again and opened the small box.

"See? It's just squares of wood, that's all," she blushed, "but I really did appreciate yer help."

"Well, that's what I am here for, and to add awesome good looks to the room, of course," he laughed.

Chappell laughed, too, as she always did in his presence. His world was so foreign to her, and there were many times that she longed to experience it with him. But how? As much as she enjoyed his wit and humor and talent, there was always in the back of her mind the reality that she was already tied to a man, that she had children with that man, and that she would be forever with that man because to leave him would be wrong, just wrong. To entertain thoughts of another man, to enjoy his company to the degree that Chappell enjoyed Dr. Turner's company, was also exceedingly wrong, so she reigned in her heart and bolstered her boundaries. She loved the tender and attentive treatment that this man gave her, but was wise enough, even in her grief, to realize that nothing could come of it. He was simply one of many counselors at this wonderful facility there to help her find her way, and then to send her back into her world again armed with philosophies to endure, to overcome, to survive, and maybe even to enjoy life.

Dr. Turner studied Chappell's face. She was an unusual woman in that she was obviously attracted to him, as many of the young female patients were, yet had the fortitude not to let it control her decisions or behavior. She was able to keep a certain respectable distance from him while maintaining a comfortable working relationship. He was not sure what to think about this. After all, pretty swooning women were quite a boost to his ego, and though he was careful never to allow anything to come of his casual flirting, he nevertheless enjoyed knowing that he was desirable.

How would he ever know if he had made that kind of impression on this woman if she always kept so aloof?

She was going to leave in a few days, and he had to know if she had seen in him anything worth her notice, or was she not attracted to him at all? Sure, it was petty, but it was all he had in this business to add excitement to an otherwise lusterless job.

Dr. Turner reached for Chappell's hand, "I am going to miss you, you know," he crooned, smiling at her and leaning forward to add earnestness to his words.

Chappell's eyes widened at his touch, something that until now, she had only dreamed about, and the crimson color rose once again to her cheeks. She felt breathless and foolish and wanted to get up and run away! Nevertheless, fighting the urge to flee, Chappell took a long deep breath, looked him full in the face, and simply said, "I'm sure you will for a while, as I will miss you for a while," slowly withdrawing her hand from his grip as she spoke. Continuing, she folded both her hands neatly in her lap, "but life goes on--I with my husband and children, and you with yer job."

Dr. Turner shook his head slowly up and down in acknowledgment of her intentions. She was very cautious, this one, and he would respect her desire to keep her admiration for him to herself.

"I wish you all the best, Chappell," Dr. Turner said, smiling, and then got up and strolled easily back out the screen door at the end of the wide hallway. She would never see him again, but she would always treasure his charm and strangeness. The fantasies of him had helped her endure four months of loneliness in this hospital of forlorn and forgotten people. Now she had to go back home: she had to step back into her world. Chappell's soft, dark waves of hair hung close to her face as she bowed her head and quietly wept.

Earl visibly trembled as he played with the band of the wide-brimmed felt hat that he held in his hands, turning it round and round on his thumb. His brother-in-law had loaned him the entire brown pin-striped suit along with the suede tie-up shoes and the chocolate brown felt hat. He felt completely stupid and out of character dressed up in these church clothes, and given a few more minutes would have squirmed out of the them and put on his work clothes which were stashed in a brown bag on the seat of his truck for just such an occasion. Before he could give it another thought, however, Earl caught a glimpse of Lydia and Darius out the corner of his eye. They were swinging like brightly colored Christmas ornaments from a branch in one of the immaculately pruned oak trees along the front walk of the huge pre-Civil War mansion that now served as a mental hospital for the state of Virginia. His face turned white with rage. He stomped down the stairs from the deep covered porch on which he had been waiting and walked briskly over to where the children were swinging, bellowing their names as he approached them.

"Darius! Lydia! Have ya' lost yer minds? Do ya' want to look like trash when yer mama sees ya'? Git down from there right now! Now, I say! You betta' both be glad you're not at home doin' this. Can't turn my back on ya'll for a second. For Pete's sake!"

Earl had reached the tree, where by this time the children had dropped to the ground, and he grabbed each child by an arm so he could shake them simultaneously, "Git to the bathroom in yonder and wash yer hands and faces, and see if ya' can't straighten yer clothes. They're yer good clothes, for Pete's sake. I shoulda' known betta' than to bring ya'll both with me. Now git!"

He pushed them forward towards the mansion, and they scrambled as fast as they could up the broad steps of the large shady porch and through the ornate screen door, tumbling into a tall handsome man as they entered who clutched them both to him laughing.

"Whoa, there! Where's the fire?"

The children stepped back staring at him with wide eyes waiting for the proverbial brick to fall and for this doctor in a white coat to firmly scold them for their lack of manners. However, he smiled at them and asked, "I assume you are here visiting someone special. Do you care to tell me the name? Perhaps I can help you find her, or is it him?"

"It's a her, and her name is Mama," Lydia beamed, soaking up his smile like a delicate flower basking in the sun's rays after months of rain.

"Shut up, Lydia!" Darius turned to the doctor. "Her name's Chappell Marshall. Ya' know which room she's in?"

The doctor's smile slowly faded as he looked back and forth at each child, searching for familiar features that would bind them to their mother, and yes, there were many. The children were beautiful like Chappell: green eyes, dark wavy hair, and slender athletic builds. However, these lovely children appeared haggard and worn with a hard edge on their expressions with which he was all too familiar after working for years with the desperate, discouraged, and depressed. At that moment Dr. Turner's heart sank. It was obvious that the world in which Chappell and her family lived had been crumbling since her departure with the children probably suffering the most, and he knew Chappell in her weakened emotional state was not ready or able to nurture these children back to health either physically or emotionally. He began to regret the decision to send her home so soon.

"Yes, I know which room is hers, but I believe you might be meeting her in the parlor instead. I'll show you the way," Dr. Turner offered in an attempt to buy time for Chappell. Perhaps he should interview her one more time before sending her on her way. Perhaps it was too soon for her to leave. He would check with Dr. Winthrop before allowing the family to see Lydia.

"Well, sir, thank ya' kindly, but our dad wants us to freshen up first, so could ya' show us where the bathroom is instead?" Darius asked politely.

Dr. Turner led the children down the long hallway to two small rooms on the left near the back door of the mansion. Each child went into his perspective bathroom and shut the door. Dr. Turner then strode back up the hallway towards the mansion's entrance where he knew he would soon encounter a very important man, Chappell's husband, but he could not remember the man's first name. Nevertheless, he strode methodically onward until he reached the screen door where he stood gazing through the mesh towards the beautiful oak trees from which was walking a very dapper looking man with his face toward the grass as if looking for something. No, he was in deep thought and deliberately stepping around the larger clumps of grass to rest his feet on more solid and shorter cropped grass, perhaps to keep the dew off his suede shoes. The poor man looked worried and gaunt and much out of place as if his shoes did not fit his feet and his attire was foreign to him. If the man had known that he was being observed from afar, he would have been embarrassed; had he known that he was being studied by the man whose touch made his wife blush, he would have been devastated.

Earl made his way slowly towards the steps of the porch, and as he climbed the stairs, he looked up at the man behind the screened door. Something about the man made the hair stand up on the back of Earl's neck, and he kept his eyes on him as he ascended the stairs to the porch. The man pushed the screened door open for Earl so that Earl could see the man's white coat. He was a doctor! Earl lowered his guard and smiled genuinely at the man who by this time was holding out his hand to him in a gesture of courteousness. Earl grasped the man's hand in a hardy handshake at which the man winced and responded by gingerly pulling his fingers from Earl's clutches as Earl vigorously shook his hand. The lack of mutual response made Earl a bit self-conscious, and he wished he had not been so eager to be friendly in front of this stranger who had now stepped back and was scrutinizing Earl with his eyes half-closed and his head turned to the side.

"Dr. Turner," he introduced himself finally, smiling perfunctorily and adding, though he knew why the man was there, "May I assist you in any way?"

The doctor's smile and mannerisms made Earl's shackles rise again. He could not put a word to it, but felt that the man was looking down on him in some way, and Earl was suddenly acutely aware of the way in which he was dressed and of his ill fitting shoes. He tossed the brown felt hat onto a nearby guest chair.

"I'm here to see my wife and to take her home with me and the kids," he began, "and I would be obliged, sir, if you would tell me where I might find her," Earl said articulately, weighing every word.

Dr. Turner looked Earl up and down again slowly, and then flashed his fake smile, gesturing with his outstretched arm towards the parlor's curtained French doors, "Right this way, please, Mr....?"

"Marshall. Mr. Earl Marshall," he said through pursed lips.

"Mr. Marshall, I will go and inquire of your wife's availability to see you. If you would be so kind as to wait here in the parlor, I will be back as soon as possible."

"What do ya' mean 'availability'? I was told to come today. I was told that I could take her home today. We drove four hours to git here, and we ain't going back without her," Earl was trying to have power over his strong voice and to not appear to be losing control, but the quick doctor seized the opportunity to debase.

"We have many disturbed and needy patients in this hospital who do not need to hear someone yelling, Mr. Marshall…"

"I'm not yellin', and you know it!" Earl countered, leaning into the doctor menacingly. He sensed what Dr. Turner was trying to accomplish with his demeaning mannerisms, and now he had backed the doctor towards the door with his strong words, demanding with his own perfunctory smile, and with a voice soft as a whisper but firm as steel, "Now you just need to go and fetch my wife."

Dr. Turner, in his practice, was not accustomed to meeting people who were neither affected by his dominance, nor by his intimidation. The verve of this poorly educated, ridiculously dressed, backwoods man, coupled with his strong good looks and steely eyes, turned the tables on Dr. Turner, and he found himself the target of a bullying from which he could not defend himself. No wonder Chappell found him, the good doctor, resistible. Though she may have been impressed by his suaveness, the doctor's haughty and flirtatious manner was no match for the strong, undaunted spirit evident in her husband. Dr. Turner left the room humiliated and defeated, but rather than going to Dr. Winthrop's office to plead for more healing time for Chappell, he went serenely to the nurse's station in the east wing.

Leaning across the top of the counter, Dr. Turner grinned coyly at the attending nurse and said, "Could you please send an aide to fetch Mr. Marshall's wife? Mr. Marshall will be waiting in the parlor, and while you are at it, there are two mongrel children wandering the hallway wreaking havoc. Could you be a dear and please have them escorted to the parlor, also. I'll owe you big time, honey."

"Whatever you say, Doctor," the nurse crooned at him.

It no longer mattered to him whether or not this frail family would survive, only that he would be rid of all reminders of this embarrassing and revealing moment. Dr. Turner turned and strolled easily and triumphantly out the back screen door.

One could hear the breathing of each individual in the little parlor; such was the tension and quietness in the room. Lydia looked back and forth between her father, who nervously fingered the band of his brown felt hat while beads of perspiration formed on his forehead, and her mother, who sat with her hands folded in her lap, gazing down at the floor with no expression on her face. Chappell had not acknowledged any of them since she entered the room ten minutes earlier. Darius' face was full of hurt and confusion as he stared at his mother, waiting for her to at least look at him and smile. Why was she not glad to see him? He had not done anything wrong. This strangeness was maddening, and he finally got up and stomped out of the room, going out to the porch to plop down on the beautiful, white wicker swing.

Lydia began to tremble in her attempt to keep from crying. She stood up and walked toward her mother. Earl glared at her with warning in his eyes, but Lydia ignored the ominous glare and kept approaching Chappell, reaching out with her hand and touching her mother's shoulder. When Chappell did not look up or move from her position, Lydia leaned over and hugged her mother, crying on her shoulder, longing for some show of recognition and acceptance. Still Chappell did not move.

"Git back from her! Can't ya' see she's not ready for all that?" Earl pushed Lydia back and kneeled down on the floor in front of Chappell. He took her hands in his and smiled at her as best he could.

"Honey, it's time to go now. Come on. Let's get yer things and go home."

Chappell finally looked up and into his eyes, but showed no acknowledgement of his intensions until he reached to take her small suitcase. At that moment, she grabbed it from him and held it to her chest for inside it was her precious jewelry. Earl did not understand what she was doing, but was glad for a proverbial sign of life, so he let her carry it as he stood her up and walked her out of the parlor with his hand around her waist.

Lydia was still standing where she had been pushed, waiting for someone to invite her to join them and be a part of this remarkable family so full of eccentricity and confusion. A chill ran up her spine as she watched her mother and father walk away, for she knew that her hopes of everything being back to normal were dashed. For four months she had anticipated this visit when she and her mother would be reunited: when her mother could show her father that everything was okay, that the family was not ruined after all. What was happening? Nothing had changed. Her mother and father were both turning their backs on her and walking away. Would they notice if she did not follow them to the truck? Would they just keep driving and get home and go back to living their miserable lives and never notice that she was not there? She felt a hand on her elbow.

"Let's go, Lydia," Darius led her out the wide screened door, down the flower-lined walk, and into the back of the old pick up truck. "It's her first day back with us, ya' know? Maybe she'll be betta' afta' we get home."

Yeah. Maybe things will be better, Lydia dared to hope. She laid her head on a sack of grass seeds and, crying, fell asleep to the swaying and bouncing of the truck on the long trip home. Darius put his coat over Lydia and then hunched down in the corner of the truck bed against a bail of rope and closed his tear-filled eyes.

Chapter Three

For the next eight years, Lydia's life and the life of the family moved in the same obnoxious, dysfunctional cycle year after year with each member of the household moving numbly from daylight existence to night time survival back to daylight existence again. Chappell did not step back into her motherly or wifely duties, so Lydia could not once again be a nine year old little girl, nor could Darius resume his eleven year old boy life. Except for the knowledge that their mother was actually living under the same roof, everyone's life continued as it had been for the four months prior to Chappell's return. The only difference was that a new and debilitating element had been added to the already peculiar existence.

During the day, Chappell stayed in her bedroom, the little bedroom off the side porch into which she had decided to move the day of her arrival back home. Earl had been visibly upset about not having his wife back in his bed where she belonged but, under the circumstances, did not feel that he could upset her anymore than she already was; so he conceded and helped her move all her things (clothes, pictures, memoirs, and other little belongings) into her new room. At that point, Chappell shut the door on them all, coming out only to place her portable porcelain potty outside the door to be emptied and cleaned every morning by Lydia, and to receive her tray of food twice a day. Otherwise, she stayed in that room sitting on the bed picking at the tiny pieces of yarn on the chenille bedspread, occasionally mumbling to herself about unseen things. Often she slept during the day which gave her energy for the bizarre nightly routine on which she commenced a few days after returning.

Earl was so in love with his beautiful wife that he would endure any hardship if it would make her happy; however, even he was not prepared for the transformation of his tender, compassionate Chappell into the loathsome creature she had become upon returning home. At first, he would go gently into her room after work to talk to her and try to repair the relationship that was so dear to him and so necessary for him to survive, but after only a few minutes, Chappell would become agitated and run him out of the room with angry screams and flailing fists. Earl was so bewildered and crushed by this behavior that he would often skip supper and retire early to his room for the evening.

One night, several days after her return--after supper was done, and the children had cleaned up the kitchen, finished their homework, and fallen exhausted into their beds-- Chappell came out of her room. She crossed the back porch and quietly turned the knob to the kitchen door, entering, and standing still in the kitchen for a moment before proceeding to the bedroom door that led to Earl's room. Opening the door, Chappell could see Earl lying there in the iron rail bed clutching a pillow to his chest and breathing rhythmically. She crept to the side of the bed and stared down at him, leaning into the side of the mattress to look into his face. The sudden movement of the mattress startled Earl who jumped up and grabbed Chappell by the wrists. Squealing, she broke free from his grip. Earl was baffled and stared at her with his heart racing. Had she come back to him?

"What are you doing here? Are you okay? Do you need something?" Earl was climbing shakily out from under the covers, unnerved by his wife's sudden and unexpected appearance.

"Chappell, do you need me?" He put his hands on her arms and would have drawn her to him, but she pushed herself away and went to a chair on the other side of the room. Earl slowly sank back down on the bed, blinking hard to hold back the tears; she was so fetching in her nightgown with her long dark hair cascading over her shoulders.

Chappell's brow began to furrow in anger, and she stood up and shook her fist at Earl screaming, "Why? Why weren't you more careful?"

Earl hung his head. Was that what this visit was about: to lay blame on him for what had happened months earlier? Had he not suffered enough for that? Earl listened with his head down and shoulders slumped as Chappell railed at him for the next hour, resting only long enough to gather more bitter thoughts before assailing him again. Only when Earl lay back on the bed and cried did she finally stop, and just as stealthily as she had entered the room, she left it.

This would begin a pattern of nightly anguish that would go on for eight years. On the first night, Lydia had crept up and listened with her ear pressed tightly against the door, intent on hearing every harsh word hurled at her father. She felt a twinge of guilt at the pleasure she felt listening to his debasement by Chappell, like it was pay back for the mental and emotional torture through which he had put Lydia, but after a little while, she could not bear to hear anymore. No one deserved so much dirt being flung at them, so much blame being heaped on them, and for what? Her mother would never come right out and say. Because there was still a modicum of respect and love for her father in the deepest recesses of her heart, Lydia did not want him to feel the unbearable pain of rejection with which she herself had been living. After the first night, Lydia would not get out of bed to listen, but would stay in bed and try to go back to sleep. She wondered if Darius was ever awakened by the nightly yelling and screaming in their father's room. If he was, he never mentioned it to Lydia, not in all those eight years.

Earl endured the nocturnal abuse of his wife because she was so convinced in her mind that all that had happened was his fault. He loved Chappell and would not fight back. If this was what it took to make her well and be herself again, then he would endure it, and he did-- night after night, year after year. He learned how to cat nap during the screaming, at least until she shook him and woke him back up. He took naps during lunch at work, and went to bed right after supper at night. Every night he tried to listen to her more closely to see if there was any improvement in her words or attitude towards him and the family. Every night he cursed the doctors who had let her go too soon. Every night he grew wearier than the night before.

One Saturday, during the eight years of eccentricity, when Lydia had just turned ten years old, Earl came into the kitchen where Lydia was boiling cabbage and making cornbread. He stood there a few moments watching her, though she knew by now not to look up at him lest he go off on a rampage about something. Then suddenly he grabbed her by the arm, lifted her up in the air, and swung her over to the table where she sat with her legs dangling over the edge. He had Chappell's large sewing scissors in his right hand.

"Dad, what're ya' doin'?" cried Lydia as he grabbed a hunk of her beautiful long hair and held it up to cut it.

"I'm tired of ya' walkin' 'round here with yer hair half washed and half combed, and Darius is too old to be helpin' ya' wash it. It don't look right for a boy to be doin' stuff like that. So I'm cuttin' it short, and then you can wash it betta' and I don't hafta' look at it."

"But mom wants my hair long," she pleaded holding onto his wrist and weeping uncontrollably.

"Well, yer mom ain't out here helpin' ya' with it, is she? In fact, she ain't out here helpin' any damn body with any damn thing, is she? So I reckon I make the calls now, and I say it goes!" and with that proclamation he whacked off a huge hunk of Lydia's long, soft wavy hair and threw it onto the floor. She shrieked in horror!

Darius was coming into the back porch with a load of wood when he heard Lydia's blood curdling scream. He dropped the wood into the box and ran into the kitchen.

"Lydia! Dad?! What're ya' doin'? Are ya' crazy? Mom would neva' cut her hair like that!" Darius had picked up a huge lock from the floor and was staring at it incredulously.

"Well, I'm not yer mom, and if ya' don't get the hell outa' here and mind yer own business, you'll be next, only I'll use my razer on yer sorry meddlin' head. Now git!" Earl placed his boot on Darius' stomach and pushed him hard out the kitchen door.

Darius was so furious he could not breathe. He banged on his mother's door.

"Mom! Mom! Ya' gotta' do somethin'! Ya' gotta' stop Dad. He's hurtin' Lydia! Mom?!" But there was no response from inside the little room.

Darius plopped down on the wood box determined not to leave the house. He listened as his father relentlessly chopped off Lydia's hair amid her cries of terror and hated himself because he was too small to take on his father. Poor Lydia, he thought, how much more could she endure? Can pure hate actually kill a child? If so, his sister's days were numbered on this earth. Darius listened a little longer, and then a thought came to him.

"Now that's betta'. I expect to see yer hair clean and combed all the time now, ya' hear? Ya' won't be makin' a laughin' stock outa' me by the way ya' look. You neva' was perty or nothin', so yer hair bein' short shouldn't make a bit of differnce to ya'. If ya' eva' was perty, it might be differnt." Earl threw the scissors on the table. "Now clean up this mess and finish fixin' suppa'."

As he walked through the porch to the back door, Earl looked at Darius, "I'm goin' to the store. Git yer chores done," and he left.

"Yessir," Darius said through gritted teeth and stomped out the back door.

In that moment, Lydia appeared in the kitchen doorway. She gazed at her mother's door in disbelief, and then went to pick up the little sliver of a mirror that lay on the side table where the porcelain wash bowl was kept. Upon looking at her chopped up hair, Lydia wept and trembled and could not believe what her father had done to her. How ugly she was! At least her hair had given her some beauty. Why did he do this? As she was sobbing at her reflection, Lydia could see in the mirror that her mother's door was opened a crack, but as she watched, the door gently closed shut again. In that moment, Lydia began to hate her mother and wished that Chappell had just died instead of going to that hospital. Life would be so much more bearable. Maybe Daddy would still be angry at her, but maybe he would not. Maybe if Mom had gone for good, Dad could have learned to love what he had left and gone on. Lydia turned suddenly, and running to her mother's door, kicked it over and over as furiously as she could, rattling the hinges.

"I hate you, ya' hear?! I hate you!" Lydia went back into the kitchen to clean up her locks of hair. She put as many of them as she could in a small brown paper bag which she hid under her mattress. One day, when her hair was long again, she would throw away the beautiful locks of hair, but for now, they were her promise to herself to be beautiful when she grew up. She would show him; one day lots of men would think she was beautiful.

Darius waited for his father to drive away in the old truck before going back into the house. He saw Lydia sweeping the last remnants of hair off the floor and leaned down to hold the pan for her to sweep the mess into it. He opened the fire box on the wood cooking stove and threw in the lovely remnants of hair. Burning hair has a peculiar smell anyway, but today, the stench was particularly sickening.

"Come with me," Darius said picking up the scissors from the table.

Lydia numbly obeyed her brother, and they both headed out behind the wood shed where Darius sat Lydia on a stump and looked down at her head.

"Look. I'm no barber or nothin', but I think I can make yer hair look a little betta', ya' know, a little less choppy. I always watch Mr. Davis when he does my hair, so maybe I can shape up yer head a little. Ya' think?"

Lydia looked up at her brother with so much gratitude and trust that he had to blink away a tear before beginning the task of salvaging her femininity. It took about twenty minutes, but when he was through, she actually looked rather cute and pixie-like. Darius put the scissors in his pocket.

"There. That really is betta'. The guys are gonna' tease ya', but maybe we can come up with a story 'bout it, ya' know, like you was attacked by a mountain lion, and he pulled yer hair out so bad that we had to cut it off."

"My scratches are gone, though, and besides, when was the last time anybody saw a mountain lion 'round here? No, I'll just tell 'em I wanted it short myself. I don't care anymore who laughs or not. They already laugh at our clothes and the cardboard in our shoes. What's one more laugh gonna' do?

Darius looked at his sister. She was so wise to be so young, and she was right. Their clothes were worn by at least four or five cousins before they got them, and by the time the shoes were handed down to them, they had to put cardboard in the bottoms to cover up the holes and try to keep out some dirt. When it rained, though, their feet got soaked and cold and muddy. Lots of kids at school found this amusing, and Darius and Lydia had learned to ignore it most of the time, but for a girl to go around in public with a boy haircut, well, there was going to be proverbial heck to pay.

That night passed like any other, and the next day Lydia and Darius trudged down the dirt road to the bus stop as usual, bracing for the worse that could happen. The bus ride was a nightmare with the bus driver allowing the children to torment Lydia mercilessly until they arrived at school. Darius got off the bus and looked at Lydia.

"Ya' gonna' make it?"

She shook her head yes.

"Yell if ya' need me," He headed to his classroom.

"Darius!" Lydia called to her brother, "Thanks for everything."

Darius nodded his head and went to class. Lydia did likewise.

"My goodness, Lydia! What happened to your hair?" her teacher exclaimed. "It looks like a boy's hair cut. Did you have an injury or something?"

Lydia thought a moment, and then said, "Yeah, I was climbin' through the barbed wire fence to get away from Lucinda-- our cow?--and my hair got so tangled that I had to get cut free. Lucky for me that I was on the outside of that fence away from Lucinda, or she might a' stomped me good!"

The students gathered around her and sadly touched her hair, offering her condolences and reassuring her that it would grow back out quickly. In the meantime, they all agreed that her haircut was kind of cute and suited her face, but of course, the long hair suited her even more. Lydia felt triumphant for the first time in a long time. Maybe it was okay to lie sometimes, at least when the circumstances were such that the truth could not be revealed. Anyway, it was nobody's business but her own, right?

Chapter Four

It was the last day of school and Lydia could not wait to get on the bus and head home for the summer. The children around her were hugging each other and wiping tears from their eyes because they would not see each other for a long time--three whole months. Lydia kept a distance from the other children. She had no desire to hug anyone, nor for anyone to hug her. Such displays of emotion could not possibly be real; no one could care that much about someone else, especially someone who was not a family member. Even the sight of Darius did not invoke in her the desire to hug him, and he was family. She did look up to him and greatly appreciated the times that he seemed to step in for her and try to protect her, or at least try to make up for the harm that had been done to her. However, the thought of touching each other, hugging each other, repulsed Lydia to the point of shuddering.

"Lydia, I'm going to miss you this summer," her teacher smiled and laid a hand on Lydia's shoulder.

"Yes, ma'am," she said and ever so slightly squirmed out from under the touch. "I'm gonna' miss you, too," Lydia replied perfunctorily. The truth was that she would be glad to get away from this teacher who seemed so clueless: who enjoyed putting a dunce cap on Lydia's head and sitting her in the corner when she caught Lydia sleeping, or when her homework wasn't done, or when she did not know an answer. She was just one more nemesis in Lydia's life, another blind and self-centered person doing her job but nothing more. The bus pulled up at that moment, and Lydia turned away from her teacher and boarded.

Darius was still getting pats on the back from his buddies when the bus pulled up, and Lydia was afraid that he would be goofing around and get left behind.

"Git on the bus, Darius!" she called from an open bus window. He looked up and the smiled faded from his face. Reaching down and grabbing his book bag, he trudged onto the bus and sat down beside Lydia.

"It's not like they're gonna' leave me or nothin'. I'm not gonna' see those guys all summa', ya' know."

"Sorry," Lydia apologized. The last thing she wanted to do was get Darius upset with her at the very beginning of the summer. She made a mental note never to call him down again for anything, not even if his life depended on it.

The bus bumped and jostled along the back country roads, stopping every mile or so to let a few people off, then finally came to a halt at the end of the Marshall's long dirt drive.

"See you kids next fall!" the bus driver happily announced as the two children stepped off the bus. "Take care, now!" and he drove merrily away.

Darius turned toward the house, but before he took a step, he heaved a long slow sigh. Lydia looked up at him, wondering what was the matter, and then looked towards the house to see what she was missing. There in the shade of the old oak trees in the yard was Earl's truck.

"Man! I really wanted to have my chores done before he came home today so I could maybe go out in the woods before he got here and relax a little before supper."

"Maybe ya' still can."

"No, you watch. He'll have somethin' planned to take up my whole evenin'. Hell, he prob'ly has the whole summa' planned with extra work for us both to do so we can't have no time to ourselves."

"You're not supposed to use that word, Darius," Lydia scolded, but then she remembered her mental note. "I'm sorry. I won't neva' say that again, I promise," she declared and pulled on his hand to get him to answer.

"Forget it," he muttered and headed toward the house.

Earl was sitting at the kitchen table with a cup of coffee that he apparently had made for himself as the dull tin coffee pot had been cleaned by Lydia that morning before she went to school. He did not look up when the children came into the room.

"You kids are gonna' go live with yer grandma and aunt for awhile. Lydia, you're gonna' help yer grandma at the barn stringin' leaves and anythin' else she needs, ya' hear?"

Lydia nodded, not looking up.

"Darius, you're gonna' go help yer aunt in the fields pullin' 'bacca and doin' other stuff 'round the farm as she needs it."

"But, Dad, what about this place?" Darius asked, not wanting to leave his own home for the entire summer. "What about the summa' vacation? Don't we get one?"

"What the hell do ya' need a summa' vacation for? What you takin' a vacation from, I wonda'? I don't want to hear no more 'bout it. Since I took this job with the tractor company, I ain't been farmin', so there's no need to have the both of ya' runnin' 'round here outa' control. Now git' yer things togetha'. I don't have all day. I gotta' get back to work and make up this time I'm wastin' gettin' ya' both to the farms. Go!" Earl bellowed as he pushed back his chair and stood up to go outside. "I want ya'll out to the truck in five minutes, ya' hear?

Darius was fuming! He stomped into the bedroom and slammed the door on Lydia as she was about to enter.

"Let me in! I gotta' pack, too," she demanded.

The door was flung open hard and fast, and Darius was standing there clutching the doorknob, glaring at Lydia, seething with disgust.

"Ever' time I turn 'round you are ruinin' my life! Why can't he just punish you? Why do I always hafta' be dragged into it? I wish you'd died a couple of years ago. I wish you'd died! Then I could've lived a normal life for a change. I wish she'd died, too," he motioned with his head towards his mother's door. "The both of ya'

are nothin' but trouble to me, now git outta' here and let me pack!"
He slammed the door in Lydia's face.

Lydia was dumbfounded. He was her last ally on this earth.
If he felt this way--if he had always felt this way—then how utterly
and entirely alone she was. Uninvited tears ran in torrents down her
face. She stood frozen to the spot, not knowing what to do. Earl was
waiting for them both to be ready in five minutes, but she did not
dare to remind Darius of this. She had made a mental note not to
ever again call him down for anything, and she was not going to go
against it, even if meant a beating by her father. She would wait
until Darius opened the door and let her inside.

Within a few minutes, the door swung open fast, slamming
the handle into the wall, bouncing back again to close, but Lydia
stopped it with her hand. Pushing past her without a word, Darius
headed for the truck with his gunnysack full of clothes that he
would probably outgrow before the summer was through. Lydia
watched him leave out the door, and then went sadly into the room
to quickly gather her belongings in her own burlap sack. She was
about to leave when she remembered the brown bag of beautiful
hair. Reaching far under the mattress, Lydia fished around with her
hand to find the treasured bag, but it wasn't there!

"Lydia! Git out here, now!" Earl roared.

"I'm comin'!" Lydia yelled back, but she was not about to
leave without the brown bag. With all her tiny frame and might,
Lydia heaved the thick, heavy ticking mattress off the bed frame

and left it in a heap on the floor. The brown bag of hair was not there.

"Lydia, if I hafta' call ya' agin', I'm takin' off my belt!"

Lydia ran out of the bedroom door with her sack of clothes, taking a running leap out the back screen door, bypassing the few steps, and landing sprawled on the ground below. She quickly got up, brushed herself off, and continued running to the truck, climbing in over the closed tail gate. Earl had already started the truck and began pulling off as Lydia was climbing into the back, flinging her onto her brother who was sitting propped up near the truck window. He heaved her off of him.

"Sit over there," he spit out at her, pointing to a pile of rope a few feet away from him. Lydia obeyed submissively, still baffled about the bag of hair. Where could it be? She knew she had left it under the mattress. Had her father found it and thrown it away? Lydia lowered her head so her brother could not see her crying. That bag had been so special; it contained a promise. Was this a sign from God that she would never be beautiful? Did even God hate her? If so, for what? She still did not know what she had done wrong, and nobody would talk about it.

A pair of tender, longing, moist eyes watched as the old rusty mint green truck rolled away down the long dirt drive towards the gravel state road that would take her children to the homes of their relatives for the long hot summer. Chappell clutched her daughter's soft beautiful curls to her heart, stroking them gently, watching as the truck disappeared around a curve into the shadows of the trees along the state road. She crooned an old song softly to herself as she stroked the hair:

'Sweet and low... sweet and low. Winds of the southern seas.
Blow, blow, soft and low. Winds of the southern seas.'

Chappell hummed a few bars as she tried to remember the rest of the words to the song she used to sing years ago when she was nursing her babies and rocking them to sleep. She hummed softly, watching up the road, tenderly fingering the long locks of hair. Then the last few words came to her, and she sang:

'Bring my love safely home to me, while my little ones,
As my little ones ...sleep.'

"Please don't hate me, Lydia," Chappell pleaded with trembling voice as she held the locks in front of the window, letting the afternoon sun bring out the amazing shine and auburn highlights of her daughter's beautiful hair. She meticulously placed the hair back in the brown bag and slid it under her mattress for safe keeping. It was going to be a long, lonely, hot summer. Who would empty her potty?

Lydia was dropped off first at her grandmother's house. This was Chappell's mother, and she walked briskly out the door and into the yard to meet them as they drove up and parked.

"Hello, hello, hello! My goodness! I haven't seen you two in so long that I wouldn't recognize ya' in a dark barn. Come on in! You're bound to be hungry. Earl, git their bags and ya'll come on inside. I fixed some ham and chicken both for ya', and some of my veggies straight outa' the garden. And wait 'til ya' taste my biscuits! I been using oil instead of lard, and they come out so fluffy ya' have to tie 'em down to keep 'em from floatin' plum away!" Granny kept babbling about one thing after another almost the entire meal, leaving precious little for anyone else to say. When the meal was done, Earl rose to leave.

"Lydia can help ya' with these dishes and all. I'm beholdin' to ya' for takin' her in this summa'."

"Well, Lydia, I'll leave ya' to the dishes, and Darius, I'll let ya' bring me in a porch full of wood for the night, then you can meet yer dad out front at the truck. I'm gonna' walk yer father out to the truck and do my goodbyes. I'll be right back."

Earl and Granny walked out the front screen door onto the low flat rock porch. He knew what she was going to ask and dreaded having to explain how things were with him and Chappell.

"She still not comin' outa' her room?"

"No, ma'am," he lied. Nobody but the children knew about Chappell's night time rampages, and he knew the children would not talk about it. He had made sure about that long ago.

"What're ya' goin' to do 'bout it, Earl? How much longa' can you and she go on like this? Why can't ya' let me talk to her or somethin'? Maybe she would listen to me."

"Don't ya' think I tried to git her to git help? I offered for her to talk to you or anybody else she wanted, but she won't come outa' the room for anybody. She won't even talk to the children. I don't know what to tell ya', Granny. I'm doin' the best I can," he said and rubbed his hand over his forehead.

"I know ya' are, son," Granny smiled and put her arm around his shoulders. "It's just gonna' take more time, that's all. You be patient. God will do somethin' one day in His own good time. You watch. Everything will be okay one day."

"God? Ya' really still think he gives a…"

"Don't ya' say it! You just wait and watch."

Darius came around the corner of the small, dovetailed log house and stepped onto the cool stone porch. "Wood's done."

"Thank ya', son. Now you and yer father git on the road. Ya'll still have a ways to go before dark. Darius, you're a good boy. Stay that way," Granny hugged him around the shoulders.

Lydia was up to her elbows in sudsy water when she heard the familiar roar of her dad's truck. She ran to the window, dripping bubbles as she went, and leaned out in time to see her dad and brother driving away. Darius was sitting in the back of the truck.

"Darius! Bye! Bye, Darius!" she waved her arm as hard as she could. He looked at her blankly, but never waved or smiled back.

Lydia was still at the window looking sadly after the truck when her grandmother came into the room.

"Girl, look at these suds! Let's get 'em cleaned up before somebody slips up on 'em. Most everybody will be back from the barns soon. Let's make sure they have dishes to eat on."

"Who all lives here, Granny? Where'll I sleep?" It was a legitimate question as the tin-roofed log house had only one main room, a lean-to kitchen, a screened back porch, and an attic with one tiny window at each end.

"Well, let's see. You can sleep in the attic with yer two cousins, Carla and Dahlia. I don't think they'll mind having ya' around. Yer cousins, Paul and Reese, sleep in a hammock on the back porch. They're both in high school now, and I reckon they're old enough to take care of themselves. I sleep in that old bed in the main room. All the otha' hands sleep in the pack house or out unda' the stars."

"Wow! I didn't know ya' had so many people livin' in this ole house."

Granny laughed. "It's been a while since you or yer brother was here, Lydia. I've missed ya', child," Granny rubbed her hand over Lydia's hair. "Didn't ya' used to have long hair? What on earth made ya' want to cut it like this?"

"Is that what Dad told ya', that I wanted it like this?"

"Well, he never really said. Yer daddy's got a lot on his poor troubled mind right now. Ya'll need to be patient with him, Lydia. It'll all work out in time."

Yeah, when I'm dead, she thought, and turned to finish the dishes before the unfamiliar horde of people bombarded the kitchen in search of food.

Chapter Five

Lydia remembered all her cousins, though it had been several years since she had seen them. Dahlia was 13 years old, and her older sister, Carla, was 15 years old. They were both tall, pretty, blonde, laid-back girls, and Lydia soaked up their ambiance like a sponge, stealthily emulating their mannerisms, hoping to make it real in her life. It was like breathing fresh sweet air for the first time in years, and the two cousins seemed genuinely happy to help Lydia grow into the lady she wanted to be.

By this time, Lydia's hair had grown a few inches, and she had added a couple of inches to her height, also. That first night in the attic of Granny's house, Carla looked at Lydia with a laugh and said, "We gotta' get this girl a bra!"

Lydia, mortified, looked down and saw the two tell-tale bulges under her shirt. Could it be true? Could she need a bra already? None of the other girls at school were wearing one.

"Yes, sweetie, ya' need one right now," Carla jumped up from her place on the floor where she was painting her nails, and pulled open a drawer on an old wooden chest where clothes were kept that the two girls had outgrown. She reached around under a pile of clothes and pulled out a dingy, stringy object and handed it to Lydia.

"You can have this one for now. Let's see if it fits ya'."

As Carla reached to pull off Lydia's shirt, Lydia shrieked and ran from her.

"What's the matta'? Ya' gotta' put this on unda' yer shirt, silly! Oh, I know, you're embarrassed. Well, we'll turn 'round. Dahlia, turn 'round so Lydia can try this on."

Lydia looked at the strange object, not knowing which end should go up. Carla sneaked a peak around and noticed her puzzled look.

"Here. It goes like this," she explained as she deftly held it up by the straps, "and it hooks in the back, but we hook it in the front, and then turn it 'round to the back, ya' see?" she demonstrated in the air. "Now, go ahead and put it on," she giggled.

Lydia followed the unusual instructions as best she could, finally getting the awkward thing arranged and pulling her shirt back down over it. Never in all her days had she worn such an unpleasant article of clothing. Was it really necessary?

"Do I really hafta' wear this awful thing?"

The two girls burst out laughing, and then took her hands and they danced around in a little circle singing, "Lydia's a woman! Lydia's a woman!"

"You'll be havin' a visiter soon, ya' know," Dahlia prophesied with a smile as they settled down on the thick quilt pallet on the floor. "I got my visiter just last month, but ya' must be gonna' start soona' than me."

"Whatta' ya' mean? Who is it?" Lydia asked apprehensively, hoping it would not be her father.

"It's not a who, it's a what," laughed Dahlia. "Yer period! Ain't yer mama ever told ya' 'bout all that?"

"No, she's neva' talked to me 'bout nothin' like that."

The two sisters looked wide-eyed at each other, and then took it upon themselves to explain to Lydia all they knew about the subjects of puberty, periods, babies, and boys, taking turns so each one could gather new thoughts about the subjects before proceeding. The conversation continued into the night until they looked up during the subject of boys and found that Lydia had drifted into a deep and much needed sleep. The rest of the education could wait until another night. Carla covered up her little cousin and then lay down beside her on the pallet on the floor where all three girls were sleeping as there was no bed in the attic.

Down below their window, slowly swinging in the wide two person hammock, Paul lay next to Reese listening to all the girl talk drifting down from the little window above the porch and realized that his odd looking little cousin was coming into the bloom of womanhood. He noticed when they quit talking and turned down the wick on their lantern, leaving only the crickets to entertain him. A strange tingling went through his bones as a sinister thought breezed through his mind. He could hardly believe that he had envisioned such an atrocious thing, still the image lingered in his mind as he abandoned himself to sleep.

Bright and early the next morning, Granny banged heavily on the closed door at the bottom of the narrow attic stair. Lydia woke with a start! She jumped up looking for her clothes, crying because she hadn't started the fire in the stove yet, and she hadn't gotten Darius up to do his chores, and Dad would be so mad! Her two cousins lay there watching her through their sleepy eyes. After a minute, Carla reached up and pulled her back down on the pallet, holding her from behind and saying quietly in her ear, "You're not at home, Lydia, calm down. Everything's okay. Granny has the fire started, and Darius ain't here. All ya' hafta' do is lay here a minute and wake up, and then we'll all go down and eat. Okay?"

Lydia nodded, trembling, and tried to calm her breathing. What a wonderful place! What wonderful people! She lay down between Carla and Dahlia, who both put their arms over her, and smiled. Maybe God didn't hate her after all. This was going to be a great summer. Hopefully, Darius was enjoying his morning, too. Maybe there were other people to help him do his work so it wouldn't be so hard, and maybe he would get a really good breakfast for a change. Lydia sincerely hoped so.

Everyone worked together at this farm without anger, without fear, without dread. Laughing was constant and infectious, and before noon, Lydia found herself laughing as much as everyone else. Nobody got mad at her if she made a mistake, they would just show her how to do it right. Gather one, two, three leaves in a bundle, and then hold them out to the stringer in one hand while gathering up three more leaves in the other. The person stringing would tie a bundle of tobacco leaves on one side of the five foot stick with one looping swing, and string another bundle of leaves on the other side of the stick with another looping swing, so that there would be thirty-two bundles in all on one stick before it was tied up, lifted off the wooden "horse", and laid in a pile until evening. At that time, every working hand would gather at the barn, and all the sticks would be hoisted up into the two story barn to be cured for selling in the fall. Mules would be ridden back home or pull a wagon behind them on their way back to the barns, and everyone would spend the next hour pealing thick, black, sticky wax off their hands and arms to make it easier to wash up for supper, often saving the wax in a collective ball to wound up in string and use for a baseball on Sundays.

Granny always had food ready to eat at supper because she got up so early in the morning to get it ready before going to the barn. As a result, she was always asleep long before anyone else in the house. Everyone retired early to their perspective places of sleep, even if they weren't going to bed right away, so Granny's sleep would not be interrupted. A little room off the screened back porch, where Paul and Reese slept, served as a pantry and a place in which to keep a porcelain potty to use at night in lieu of trekking out in the dark to void oneself on the ground behind the pack house. During the night, the ladies of the house would use this potty, and then empty it outside in the morning.

One particularly humid midsummer night, when the attic room had become so hot during the day that even the cool night air could not lighten the burdensome heat, Lydia decided to go down to the porch and put some water on her face and neck. She believed everyone to be asleep, and so she tip-toed down the steep treacherous stair, through the main room where Granny was sleeping, past the kitchen, and out to the porch where Paul and Reese slept together in the wide hanging rope bed that could be taken down each morning and put away. One of them was snoring which amused Lydia, and she put her hand over her mouth to stifle a giggle as she gingerly opened the pantry door and reached inside for a piece of a cut up old towel to use as a washcloth.

The buckets of water were on the washstand on the other side of the porch, so Lydia got down on hands and knees to crawl under the hanging bed to get to the stand and dip some water with the tin dipper into the porcelain bowl used for washing. As she dipped her cloth into the cool water and began to wash her face, a hand touched her shoulder. Lydia gasped and turned around quickly to see Paul with his finger over his lips in a gesture that said to keep quiet. She let out a sigh of relief, and then turned around to wring her cloth out again. Paul slowly swung his legs over the side of the bed, trying not to wake up his cousin, Reese, and sat there behind Lydia watching her wash her face and neck. He leaned up and whispered quietly in her ear, "You're gettin' to be quite a lady, what with yer cute figure and all."

"What? What's a figure?" Lydia whispered back.

Paul looked around at Reese to make sure he was still asleep, and then motioned for Lydia to come with him. They moved stealthily past the bed, and out the screen door, making sure not to let it slam behind them. Paul motioned for Lydia to follow him, and together they walked out into the night toward the barn where the two mules were housed.

"Wher're we goin'?" Lydia asked.

"Where we can be alone," he answered with a smile.

They were entering the v-shaped opening in the mules' pasture fence when Lydia stopped. She did not like the feel of this. Something was too familiar about it, and it made the hair stand up on the back of her neck.

"I'm goin' back in," she announced and turned to leave.

"Wait, Lydia, I won't to talk to you," he said and caught her arm.

" 'Bout what?"

" 'Bout you. Look at ya'. Ya' got perty hair, a perty smile, a perty figure…"

As Paul spoke to her, he stroked her hair, ran his finger along her lips, and was rubbing her small breasts when she flung him back.

"Stop it! Don't touch me like that!"

"Wait, Lydia, you'll like it, honest. It'll make ya' feel good, and then you'll be wantin' me to do more."

He put his arm around her waist and drew her into him, kissing her and feeling her breasts. Lydia was shocked and embarrassed, but her fighting was fruitless. Why hadn't she worn any shoes? How could she kick him and get away without shoes?

Suddenly, Paul was thrown hard onto the ground, and Lydia ran as hard as she could to the house, pausing to look back only when she had reached the steps to the porch. Standing over Paul was Reese with his tight fists ready to flail Paul if he dared to fight. Lydia had never been so relieved to see someone in her life. She went hastily up to her attic room and crawled between her wonderful cousins to sleep. She would not make this mistake again.

"What do ya' think you're doin'?" Reese asked his cousin.

"Just havin' some fun with her, that's all."

"Well, next time, I'm gonna' kill ya', ya' hear?" Reese stomped back to the porch, grabbed his blanket and went out to the front porch to sleep in the wooden swing. It was a restless and uncomfortable sleep, but he could not bring himself to share the same bed with such a loathsome monster. From now on, Lydia would be under his watchful eye, and he would make sure nobody on this farm ever hurt her. If Lydia's brother was here, he would do the same thing, wouldn't he?

Granny owned only twenty seven acres of land, most of which were heavily wooded, and the ten acres that was clear, she used for pasture. As a result, she was forced to tenant other people's farms. Before her husband died, he had secured the use of several rather large farms in the area on which to raise tobacco. He and the owner of the land (usually someone who was unable to farm for themselves because of sickness, or because they found themselves with no hands to work the land) would share the profits come fall when the tobacco was sold on the open market in Raleigh. It was a good arrangement for everyone. Now that she was a widow, Granny had to keep working the land to survive, and was thankful to have so many grandchildren willing to help each year. She paid her hired hands well, and her reputation as a great southern cook drew both local and migrant workers to her door every year.

One morning, Granny roused everyone from sleep a little earlier than usual, for they were to pull tobacco at Miss Lucinda's farm this week, and it was further away than the other farms. Miss Lucinda was a widowed, retired school teacher who was too old to manage her land anymore, so she relied heavily on Granny to bring in enough profits for her to have a good winter. After breakfast, the crew of family and hired hands hitched the mules to the back of a long, wide, flat trailer loaded on one end with tobacco sticks, twine, and two tall, narrow "slides" for leaves, and on the other end with anyone who could find a place to sit for the ride. The trailer was hooked to a large red tractor.

Granny called out last minute orders to the crew, "Paul! Come here and take these bags of biscuits. Reese! Carla! Ya'll git the jugs of watta'. Dahlia! Lydia! Hold onto these baskets tight! There's cake in 'em for lata'."

Everyone was bustling to do what they were told and still get a good seat on the trailer towards the center where the bouncing was not so harsh on the spine. Lydia noticed that two of the hired men had rifles with them.

"What's the rifles for, Dahlia?" Lydia asked.

"In case an animal wanders up to us foamin' at the mouth with rabies." Dahlia said with authority.

"Really? We gonna' be that far out?" Lydia asked amazed.

"Yeah, we're gonna' be in the middle of nowhere! There ain't no roads to the fields where a truck can take, so that's why we're ridin' on this traila', and there ain't no barn, so we'll be standin' beside this thing handin' leaves. I don't like it. If we're lucky, they'll be able to park us in some shade."

The bumpy ride took half an hour, and everyone was glad to finally see the fields. Hired hands jumped off the slow moving trailer and began to haul the slides off the side as they walked, leaving them at the ends of the rows of tobacco. The trailer pulled off the beaten trail and bounced over the uneven terrain of Miss Lucinda's land, coming to a stop at the edge of a row of trees next to the closest field. The mules were unhitched from the trailer and led away to be hitched up to the slides and guided down the first few rows of tobacco. Before Granny could even slip off the wagon, Paul, Reese, and the other men were already bent over snapping off the few yellow-green leaves near the bottom of each plant as they slowly proceeded down the rows. Lydia and the other ladies were left to unload the long, narrow, wooden horses, and remove the twine and piles of bare sticks from the trailer to make room to lay sticks full of tobacco which they would haul later to Miss Lucinda's barns. They set themselves up on the side of the trailer next to the shady trees, found a cool, safe place under the tractor seat in which to store the food, and sat down to wait for the first slide full of leaves. They would go through this routine everyday for the next week.

Though there were no roads where they were, there was a train track down a hill on the other side of the farthest field. Everyday at lunch time, as the workers all sat on the trailer under the shady trees to eat, they could hear the engineer blow his jarring whistle to warn the people and animals on the route of his passage. One day, Reese, Paul, Carla, Dahlia, and Lydia decided to go sit at the top of the hill and wave at the engineer as he passed.

"Take yer food with ya'," Granny ordered. "Eat as ya' go, 'cause ya' won't have time to eat when ya' get back."

The group of cousins walked hastily toward the far hill, hoping to get there before the train passed. When they arrived, Carla and Dahlia sat down on the top of the hill to wait.

"Come on, ya'll, let's go down there," Paul shouted as he bounded down the hill.

Lydia and Reese followed behind him leaving the older girls to watch. As they got to the bottom of the hill, Paul jumped onto one of the rails.

"Be dogged if I can't feel the track vibratin'!" he shouted.

"Really?" Lydia stood on the track to feel for herself.

"Ya' know, they say that injuns out west could put their ears on the tracks and tell when a train was comin'. Let's do it!" Paul challenged looking directly at Reese.

"Alright, let's do it," Reese took up the challenge and got down on his hands and knees and put his ear on the sun warmed track.

"What're ya'll doin'? Git off that track!" called Carla from the safety of the hill.

Lydia followed Reese, getting down on her hands and knees and pressing her ear to the track.

"Can ya' hear anythin'?" asked Paul as he was going back up the hill.

"Where're ya' goin'?" Reese frowned at him.

"You heard the lady," Paul grinned and clambered back up the hill, sliding on the loose dirt until he reached the top where he sat next to Carla, still grinning.

"Stay, Reese, please? I want to try it," Lydia begged.

Reese put his ear back on the track, and together they waited for the sound or sensation of a coming train. It wasn't but a few minutes before Reese exclaimed, "I can feel it! Just a little, but I can feel it, Lydia!"

Lydia closed her eyes and listened intently. Soon her ear began to tingle from the slight vibration of the track. She turned to Reese and shouted, "I can feel it!"

Laughing, they stayed there with their ears pressed firmly to the track feeling the vibration getting stronger and stronger until they heard shouting from the top of the hill.

"Git outa' there, ya'll! It's comin'!" bellowed Carla, pointing up the track.

"Come on, you idiots! Time to stop! Now git up here!" Paul scolded, standing now with his hands on his hips.

Lydia and Reese stayed frozen to the track, not moving, even though they could see the silhouette of the train growing larger. Suddenly, Reese punched Lydia in the arm, "Come on! We did it! Let's go now," but Lydia would not budge. She was determined to stay until the last minute.

"Lydia! It's gettin' too close! Come on!" Reese had gotten up and started up the hill, but looking back he could see Lydia still hovering over the track.

"You crazy?" Reese clambered back down the hill and grabbed the back of Lydia's shirt. She shrugged him off. The ground was beginning to shake under them, and their family was screaming and crying out at the top of the hill. The train emitted a deafening blast of its whistle warning her to get away, but Lydia had to wait until the last moment, she had to beat the fear.

When the train was so close that no one's voices could be heard over the clatter of the train cars shuttling on the tracks, Reese grabbed the back of Lydia's cotton shirt and yanked her off the track, but not in time for them to climb back up the hill. The train dashed by only a few feet from them, pinning them both to the side of the hill with such a force of wind that Reese, clutching with all his might to a sassafras root sticking out of the side of the hill, was afraid that he would lose his grip on Lydia's shirt, and that she would get sucked underneath the train's grinding wheels.

For a few bizarre moments, the two cousins breathed impending death, and then suddenly, with another blast of the mighty whistle, the dull red caboose shot by, and it was over. They both crumpled to the ground, trembling violently, thankful to still be alive. Reese shakily stood up and stood there yelling at Lydia about what a stupid thing that was to do. Lydia squinted at him for a moment, then began to giggle.

"I can't hear a thing you're sayin', Reese. My ears are numb! Ya' look so funny with yer mouth movin' all around and nothin' comin' out!" she was bent double with laughter.

It was infectious, and Reese, chuckling, grabbed her in a headlock and shouted as loud as he could, "You're crazy, ya' know that? But ya' got enough nerve for the both of us. I ain't never worryin' 'bout ya' agin'"

The others had scrambled down the hill, and Carla and Dahlia ran to Lydia and hugged her to them, crying loudly and shaking all over. Paul grabbed Reese in a bear hug, and then the shaky bunch scrambled back up the hill towards the trailer, swearing oaths to each other along the way to never tell Granny about what they just did.

There were other oaths sworn that summer, like the one about swimming on Sunday in the old unused rock quarry filled with water. The cousins would dive into the murky, brackish water in their Sunday clothes unaware of the jagged edges of rock hidden beneath its surface, never knowing how closely they came to cracking a skull or breaking a bone. Afterward they would allow the bright sun to dry them off as they walked the half mile back to Granny's house, sharing any bits of information gleaned from reading that they thought the others might like to know about, or just to show off their new knowledge.

Once the adventurous cousins, on one of their Sunday ramblings around the countryside, happened upon an old abandoned school house that was established, according to the imposing wooden plaque hanging next to the door, in the year 1910, and in it were incorporated many amenities that the more modest country schools did not have, including a small gymnasium for playing ball and holding assemblies. The school was apparently built to house students from the entire surrounding area, but was abandoned years later when so many students could not show up regularly for school during the spring and fall months of tobacco season, leaving the expensive school unable to produce the academic results it promised. Later, it was replaced by smaller, established local schools, and the beautiful building was left to deteriorate under the summer suns and winter snows.

Many Sunday afternoons, Lydia and the others would invade the school to play basketball in the wonderful gymnasium, or wander about the halls reading the old bulletin boards, or enter the classrooms to see what was left written on the black boards and on old assignments that were left behind by reluctant students on that last sad day of school. The greatest treasure that they discovered, however, was the library full of books—lots and lots of lovely math, history, literature, science, and social studies books everywhere to be read on those Sunday afternoons, or acted out on the little stage at the end of the auditorium. It was their own Never-never land, and Paul was Peter Pan, always calling the shots and always suggesting what to do next, but Lydia often stayed behind and finished what she was reading while the others fantasized on stage. She found math books and worked on learning the knowledge that had passed her by during the school years, and she discovered that she was quite good at math, even math that was above her grade level. It was her favorite way to spend those restful Sunday afternoons.

It was a blessing that Lydia started her menstrual periods that summer where her female cousins could help her understand what was happening to her and help her to learn how to take care of herself during that week of bleeding. The whole summer had been a magnificent, soothing respite from her bleak and dark life, but the summer had ended, and it was time to go back home and start school. That Sunday morning, as Lydia and her Granny sat on the porch swing waiting for Earl and Darius to come to take her home, Lydia began to sweat profusely, beads of perspiration standing out on her brow. Her throat felt tight, and it became hard to breathe, so she held her head back and began to gulp air into her lungs, but her throat only tightened more. Lydia stood up and turned to her grandmother, face white and mouth gaping open, clutching her throat. Granny gazed at her for a moment not understanding what was happening, but then she jumped up and began to pat Lydia on the back.

"Lydia! Breathe!" she ordered while supporting Lydia's arm to keep her from falling.

Lydia strenuously sucked in a short breath and then began to bawl uncontrollably.

"I can't breathe! I'm gonna' die!" She gasped. "Please, Granny, I don't wanna' go home. They hate me," she wailed. "Please let me live here. I'll look after ya' all winter. I'll go to the well for ya', and cook for ya', and read to ya' at night. Please, Granny, just don't make me go home," Lydia was weeping miserably, gripping her grandmother tightly around the waist with her face buried in her shoulder.

Granny held lovingly to Lydia for a long time while Lydia poured out her distress and grief through salty tears. Soon her sobs became void of water and were nothing more than dry heaves, and then Granny took her by the shoulders and peered into her eyes.

"I wish I could help ya', Lydia, but I can't," she replied slowly. "Ya' dad needs ya' back home, and even if I could keep ya', the school bus don't run out here no more, and ya' know I don't drive that ole Ford truck unless I absolutely have to 'cause I can't git out to the station to git gas, and Lord knows how much gas it would take to git ya' to school and back every day. Lydia, angel, don't cry no more. It breaks my heart, and ya' don't want to break my heart before ya' leave, do ya'?"

Lydia looked into the smiling eyes of her grandmother for a long moment. She would memorize that expression of love and store it away in her heart and feed from it during the school year, and hopefully, maybe one day, she could live with her grandmother--one day.

That winter was particularly harsh, and Granny did not live through it, but died in February. She was buried amid a snowy graveside funeral, and lowered into the frozen ground to be covered over with clumps of sod. The family placed a small wooden marker at the head of her grave bearing the dates of her long life and a brief epitaph:

THE WORLD HAS SUFFERED A GREAT LOSS

Lydia's heart was laid to rest that day in the cold grave with her grandmother, and any assurance she had ever felt in anyone and any loyalty she had ever felt towards anyone fled forever from her soul.

Chapter Six

Over the next five summers, Lydia's father farmed her out to strangers, anyone who needed a hand pulling tobacco. She worked in the fields among foreigners, ex-cons, and other misfits who would work for less money, but she never saw her wages because it was paid directly to her father. He did not spend it on any amenities or clothes for Lydia as she could still get hand-me-downs from her cousins, so at sixteen years old, she entered high school dressed in faded, ill-fitting, old fashioned dresses accompanied by odd, scuffed shoes sporting cardboard on the inside in place of soles. Had she not been pretty, Lydia could have endured worse ridicule from her peers than she did, but because of her long, dark, thick wavy hair, and her curvy figure, the derision was sometimes curbed in lieu of curiosity. Teenage boys looked hungrily at her as she walked down the halls between classes, assuming that her scruples were as vulgar as her attire, and some dared to make passes at her in the hallway, whispering lewd remarks in her ear, or grabbing her skirt as she passed by. It was mortifying to Lydia to be treated so cruelly by these young men, and she felt devastatingly ugly and embarrassed, yet never would she lower her head as she walked by, but would glower at her attackers until they backed away.

Darius had long ago ceased sitting with Lydia on the bus, or associating with her in school. His prowess in sports had made him somewhat popular at school, and even though his apparel was no better than Lydia's, the teens only goodheartedly teased him about it, and allowed him to hobnob with them to a degree. Darius appreciated the attention and would not risk losing it by associating with Lydia. She was on her own here in this academic jungle, and as far as he was concerned, he was not his sister's keeper anymore.

Lydia never ate in the lunch room, but would take her biscuit and sit in a small hidden nook outside of the band room storage door where no one could see her if they walked by. In every classroom, Lydia took the seat furthest to the back of the room and quietly sat there looking down at her books, hoping the teacher would not call on her for any answers. It was not that she wasn't prepared with knowledge, but rather that she did not want the teacher to call attention to her, and have the class looking at her with their repugnant grins, waiting to hear her speak. When this happened, she would feel her throat tighten and not be able to breathe. Beads of sweat would stand out on her forehead and seep through her clothes. She would be unable to speak, and finally shake her head that she did not know the answer so that the teacher would move on to someone else. Of course, the student's snickers would follow and Lydia's mortification would be complete.

It did not take long each semester for the teachers, at least the compassionate ones, to realize that she was dysfunctional in the classroom and leave her alone. However, no teacher ever took her aside to delve into the reason for her incapacitation, or to offer to help in any way, so Lydia spent the first two years of high school in this solitary misery, growing physically sicker each day from the results of severe and continual stress that kept her body from digesting its food as it should, or sleeping as it should, or laughing as it should, or dreaming as it should. By the time she was in her junior year, Lydia was very thin and gaunt which only fostered her mysterious appeal to the boys around her who found her surreal, therefore, nonessential, and made them want her even more, enough to occasionally ask her out, but Lydia knew what they really wanted and would just walk away without answering.

During the first semester of her junior year, Lydia mused about dying. While the teacher droned on and on in front of the class, Lydia pictured various ways of killing herself and by Christmas had decided that hanging was the surest way to go about it, but it would take some planning. It would have to be at the end of the school year before tobacco season because she did not want to interrupt her brother's activities at the school, nor make him have to face his friends again before the end of the school year. That would give him time to get over her death and get on with his life. Also, it had to be done high up in a tree where once she stepped off the branch, there would be no way of changing her mind, nor would anyone notice her right away and pull her down before the hanging had taken effect. She would use her father's good ties because he never went to church and so would never need them anyway, and besides, if she took a rope, he would notice and come looking for her. Yes, at the end of the school year, she would end her…could she call it a life? She would end this existence that ranked little higher than a worm's. It was a good and necessary plan. What would Chappell think? What would she do? It was the first time that Lydia had thought about her mother in months.

In the second semester of her junior year, the first day back to classes after the Christmas break, Lydia found herself sitting next to a stranger in her history class. He had pitch black hair and blue eyes and was dressed like the other preps in the class with a button collared shirt, pull-over cardigan sweater, khaki pants, and the latest brand named sneakers. Sitting slouched down in his desk with his arms crossed over his chest, the new boy was reading the history text with a frown on his face as if he did not approve of what he was reading. Lydia sat looking straight down at her desk with her hands folded in her lap as usual and her textbook opened to the pages that had been assigned for homework the previous day. Though she darcd not look at him, she could tell out the corner of her eye that he had glanced at her, and then looked away again.

Most of the students were milling around the room by now waiting for the tardy bell to ring and loudly chatting about the latest social event, or exchanging sweaters and hair brushes, or franticly copying someone's homework paper because they had forgotten to do the assignment. A bouncy, bubbly, blonde cheerleader suddenly showed up beside the desk of the new boy and leaned down to look at him, obviously trying to get his attention.

"Hi, I'm Naomi, and I'm very glad to meet you! What's your name?" she smiled coyly.

"Hello, Naomi, I'm glad you're glad, and my name is David," he answered back also with a coy smile.

Naomi looked over at Lydia and then asked him, "Wouldn't you rather sit over here with us, you know, away from this corner?" she motioned with her head towards Lydia while making a slight frown.

David, still slouched in his desk and with his arms still folded over his chest, glanced next to him at Lydia and replied, "No." He looked back at the surprised cheerleader, "I like the ambience in this corner just fine. Thanks anyway," and smiled mechanically at her until she moved away, glancing back once over her shoulder at Lydia.

Lydia could not help herself. She stared wide-eyed at him until he turned once more in her direction. Their eyes met for a brief moment, and then Lydia jerked her head around, facing forward again. She was trembling and could feel the crimson tide of embarrassment rising in her cheeks, and the uninvited panic symptoms coming on, but for some reason she was glad that this boy had made the choice to sit next to her.

"You don't mind terribly if I sit here, do you?" David was leaning toward her desk, trying to see her face and look into her eyes.

To Lydia, it was an intrusive attempt to invade her space, and she turned to him and bravely said, "As long as you mind your own business."

Why had she said that? He hadn't been unkind to her, or made fun of her, or tried to embarrass her like the other boys in the school had done. Why had she presented herself to him, this handsome young man, as being someone unapproachable?

"Hey," he raised his arms in the air in a sign of surrender, "whatever you say," and settled into his slouched position again, dubiously reading his history textbook.

Lydia felt totally defeated, but what if he turned out to be just like the other boys? What if he was only acting like he was nice, but deep down inside he had a sinister plan to mortify her before her peers after winning her trust? She had read enough Shakespeare plays to learn that people were capable of treachery far beyond what anyone ever thought of them, and she had lived with her father and brother's treachery long enough to know that the plays of Shakespeare were fashioned from real life. It was better not to take any chances. This good-looking boy would be kept at bay.

Most of the days in history class, the teacher lectured about the previous night's assignment making it unnecessary for the students to actually read the pages as the teacher would inevitably give them all the information they needed, and they could just jot it down in notes to study later for tests. The good looking, new boy continued sitting next to Lydia, much to the dismay of every other girl in class, but instead of taking notes, he would be reading another book, or studying his Latin assignments. Lydia wondered how he could keep up with all the material without taking notes, and apparently the teacher wondered the same thing, for after a few weeks passed by without her catching him writing, she decided to confront the good looking and popular boy in class in front of all his peers.

"David, are you getting this down?" the teacher asked with a steady, but pleasant voice.

"Yes, ma'am, I'm getting it down."

"May I see your notes, then?"

"Well, ma'am, I'm not getting them down on paper, just in my head. I'm listening to every word you're saying, so go ahead and ask me anything."

"I prefer not to test you this way, David, in front of the whole class, but I would like for you to take out your notebook and begin taking notes from this point forward. Agreed?" She asked and tilted her head to one side to wait for his response.

"Yes, ma'am! Whatever you say, ma'am."

The classmates chortled, some giving David the thumbs up sign before turning to face the board again. Lydia glanced at David to see if he was really going to follow through with his promise, and sure enough, he had his notebook out, his pencil in hand, his eyes on the board, and seemed ready to write. Good, Lydia thought, maybe he is not a slacker after all, and she settled down in her seat again, but after a few moments, something flew towards her and landed on her desk. It was a piece of notebook paper folded to a very tiny size with her name scribbled on it in an unfamiliar handwriting, and she continued to stare at the piece of paper as if it was a snake poised to strike at her if she so much as took a breath. Who could—who would—be writing her a note like this? Finally, she looked up to see who might be waiting for her to pick up the piece of paper. Nobody was turned around.

"What are you waiting for?" someone whispered next to her. It was David, and he smiled at her and nodded his head toward the note.

Lydia froze. She had expected the note to be from one of the other students in the class, someone who wanted to say something lewd, but didn't have the nerve to say it to her face, or from the cheerleader who had gotten brushed off by David the first day of class, but the note was from the boy next to her. Her heart sank. Here we go, she thought, just like the others.

"Read it," he whispered insistently.

Just then, the bell rang, and Lydia grabbed the note, put it in her pocket, gathered her books, and walked briskly out the door without ever looking at David or acknowledging his order, and she did not stop walking until she got all the way to the hidden nook in which she ate lunch. Only then did she have the nerve to consider the note. Slowly, and with trembling hands, she began to open the note as tears of disappointment filled her eyes and spilled over onto the words on the paper. Why him? Why this handsome boy? She read:

`Lydia, where do you eat lunch? Can I join you?`

`David`

Lydia caught her breath. That was it? That was all he wanted? She began to laugh out loud, forgetting where she was and that she might disclose her secret hiding place. Lydia hugged the note to her heart. It was a good note, but could she trust that his motives for wanting to have lunch with her were honorable? All her fears came rushing back into her mind, and she began to feel angry and confused. Why did it have to be so hard? Why couldn't she just laugh and talk like everybody else and have romantic notions about boys in the manner that Carla and Dahlia had spoken of many summers ago? Oh, how she wished she could talk with them now! What should she do about this request?

Lydia took out her biscuit and while she ate, she thought about what it would be like to be able to be with David and actually talk to him face to face, and laugh with him over silly things, and be able to help him with his history homework, or for that matter, any homework. Could she possibly aspire to have some normalcy in her life after all? The longer she nibbled on her biscuit, the more hope

Lydia built up in her heart, and then the first bell rang. Lydia headed for her math class with her head in a cloud. She was passed by two girls from history class, and one of them pointed to her and said, "Look at her, the whore! No wonder David wants to sit next to her. He's just waiting until he can get his piece."

Upon hearing this remark, Lydia felt ill. Her hands began to sweat and beads of perspiration formed across her forehead. The entire hallway began to spin in front of her, and she could not catch her breath. She reached out in front of her to hold onto something, but suddenly there was only blackness.

"Can you hear me, honey?" a school nurse was tapping Lydia gently on the cheek while she held a hideous smelling capsule under her nose.

Lydia began to cough and sat up on the gurney in the nurse's station.

"How'd I get here?" she asked.

"Why, you were brought in by this nice young man after you passed out in the hallway," the nurse answered smiling and pointed to a handsome senior standing next to the gurney with his hands in his pockets. It was Darius, and he smiled sheepishly at her.

"Can't leave ya' alone for a minute, can I?"

Lydia threw her arms around her hero and held him until he gingerly put his arms around her waist. She wept on his shoulder, her body wracking with every sob. Darius couldn't take it any longer and broke down and cried with her, tightening his grip around her frail body.

"Look at ya', Lydia, you're skin and bones, and ya' can't even make it a day in school without passin' out. What happened? What can I do?" he sobbed, still holding her close to him. "Can ya' ever forgive me for walking away from ya' and actin' like such a jerk?"

Lydia couldn't speak, but he knew that he was forgiven before he even asked, for that's the kind of person she was, always there and giving, and never expecting anything good from anybody in return.

"Let's ditch this place," Darius said and helped Lydia off the gurney.

"You'll miss practice," Lydia protested.

"Don't care if I do," he replied and put his arm around her waste to steady her tottering stance.

Together they went to the office and checked out, and then Darius and Lydia walked uptown to the Woolworth's on Main Street, where they sat on the bench near the dressing rooms catching up on each other's lives, feelings, and dreams. It was a bittersweet reunion because they would soon have to catch the school bus on its way down Main Street and get off again in front of their home where they would be forced to resume the drudgery that was their lives. Lydia did not tell her brother about her plans to kill herself that summer, though to her it seemed even more necessary now than ever. He would find out soon enough.

Chapter Seven

The next day, as Lydia walked down the hallway at school, her usual taunting assailants were silent and simply watched her pass by, perhaps waiting for her to faint again, or maybe feeling that she needed a break from the ritualistic derision. Whatever the reason, Lydia did not mind being left alone for a change. The students in her history class grew hushed as she walked into the room, watching her glide quickly to her desk and sit down. She stared back at them until they finally turned around, but they continued to whisper, obviously about her.

Just before the bell rang, David strode into the room and over to his desk next to Lydia. He put away his books and took out his notebook in which to take notes, then turned to Lydia.

"I didn't know Darius was your brother," he began, and then sat there looking at her waiting for a civil response.

Lydia turned to him and smiled weakly, then turned away before she spoke.

"Yeah, he's my brother," she answered.

"Wow, small world. We're on the basketball team together. He's pretty good, you know--may stand to get a scholarship for his playing. Do you ever come to the games?"

"No, Dad won't let me."

"Not even to see your own brother play ball? Why not?"

"He just won't. Anyway, I like being home without the both of 'em around on Friday nights," she explained, and then the bell rang.

"Did you read my note yesterday?" David asked.

"Yeah, but shush now, before ya' get us into trouble," Lydia was elated to have had a real conversation with this boy who seemed genuinely nice, at least so far anyway. She could hardly keep her mind on history, and right before the end of class, another paper missile landed on her desk while the teacher's back was turned. This time Lydia hurriedly opened the note. It read:

```
Well? Can we have lunch together today?
                              David
```

Lydia could feel herself beginning to sweat and turn red in the face. She took some deep breaths and picked up her pen to write:

```
Meet me at my locker in the East wing
                  Lydia
        PS. No funny stuff
```

Lydia quickly folded the note and, at an opportune time, tossed it onto David's desk. He grabbed it and hastily opened it, then turned to her and grinned, shaking his head up and down in agreement.

When the bell rang, Lydia left the room without speaking to David. She went straight to her locker, replaced her unneeded books with books for her next three classes, grabbed her lunch bag, and stood there waiting for David to come, hoping that the crowds of students would be thinned out before he came so no one would notice them walking away together. Should she take him to her secret lunch spot, or should the two of them go somewhere visible to the other students so that no one would accuse them of making out during lunch, or worse? She wouldn't have to make that decision, as it turned out, for David had plans of his own.

"Let's go sit in the atrium, okay? It's sunny there and most of the kids will be in the cafeteria. I don't relish crowds."

"I don't usually eat in…I mean, where there are many people. I like to find a quiet spot where…I…I can be alone," she stuttered.

"Yeah, but I don't want people talking, you know? And I am not saying this to be mean or anything, but you get talked about enough already, don't you think?

Lydia turned red with shame, and turned to walk away.

"Wait, Lydia, I didn't mean to hurt your feelings. I just hear stuff, that's all. I don't like what I hear, and I decided to find out for myself what you're all about, if you'll let me."

"I don't think this is a very good idea. I'll see ya' tomorrow, David," Lydia turned and walked away, entering the ladies room before he could stop her. She stayed in the bathroom until the first bell rang for fourth period, and then as she walked out, she was startled to see David still standing there!

"What're ya' doin' still here? Why didn't ya' git some lunch for yerself?" She asked incredulously.

"I wanted to be here when you came out. Look, I like you, Lydia, and would like to have a regular sit down lunch with you where we can just talk about something besides history. Please tell me that we can have lunch together tomorrow, and then if you hate it, I'll leave you alone after that, and never bother you again. Right?"

"Alright, alright, crazy person, tomorrow for sure," she agreed laughing at him.

"You have a beautiful smile, you know," he said sweetly.

Lydia blushed and looked away, "Tomorrow," she said, and went to class.

The next day, amid stares and gaping mouths, David and Lydia left history class together and, after going to each of their perspective lockers to get lunch bags, they headed to the atrium space in the center of the cafeteria hallway where there were only a few benches on which to sit, but where there was lots of bright sunshine to enjoy, and they sat and talked about various things such as the futility of history class and the insensitivity of the student body as a whole. Lydia hardly ate anything such were the butterflies in her stomach, and her head reeled with the sound of David's voice which rang out firm and strong, yet controlled and meek. He was funny at times, and at other times very serious, and Lydia clung to every word he uttered like they were golden fruit falling from one of the small shade trees planted in the atrium. It was like being in a movie, and they were each playing the part of lovers who had finally gotten together in spite of all odds; however, in the far recesses of her heart, Lydia remained guarded knowing that this could be unreal and potentially dangerous, so amid the beautiful notes of love's ballad, there was a discordant strain that ran like a thread of pain throughout the song.

"Well, the bell's gonna' ring soon, so we betta' head back to the east wing, don't ya' think?" Lydia asked, gathering up her trash and stuffing it into her brown lunch bag.

"Yeah, but I have to ask you something, and I don't want you to get mad and stomp away or anything like you did yesterday, you promise?"

Lydia froze up. Here it comes, she thought, the ulterior motive for asking her to eat lunch with him.

"I won't, I promise," she resigned herself.

"I heard that the other day you passed out in the hallway. Some girls were saying that you might be pregnant or something. Some guys said it was because you were anorexic, you know, sick. What was it, or is it any of my business?"

"No, it's none of yer business, but I'll tell ya' 'cause I want to. I can't be pregnant 'cause I haven't been with a man in that way--never. I'm not anorexic because that means a girl don't want to eat and starves herself, and I eat whenever I get the opportunity, there just aren't many opportunities, that's all. As far as I know, I'm not sick in any way. I just heard some bad news and fainted, that's all, and it really is none of yer business what the bad news was."

He held his arms up over his head, "I surrender, chief, I won't even ask what the bad news was, but thanks for clearing all that other stuff up for me. You're a strong lady, you know, to take so much junk off everybody just because…"

"Just because what?" she pushed.

"Just because of who you are. You and Darius, you're not the same as everybody else. You don't have the money to be, yet you keep coming and taking the brunt of the stupid opinions of these stupid students when you obviously have an IQ that would blow them all away. I admire you, Lydia."

"Save it. I don't need your admiration anymore than I need their approval," she spat out nodding her head towards the cafeteria."You're a sweet guy, David, but ya' don't owe me anything, and I don't hafta' be yer charity case, so if ya' don't mind, I'd like to leave now and get ready for class."

David shook his head, and Lydia walked away alone, leaving him wishing that he could reach up in the air and snatch back all the words with which he so freely and thoughtlessly bombarded Lydia. He would make it up to her tomorrow in history class.

Lydia sat alone in the front of the bus as usual, but this time she was oblivious to the chaos and movement all around her. Even though it had ended badly, today's lunch was memorable and magical and Lydia wanted to think only about it and nothing else. For a brief moment in time, she had felt normal and average and okay, and she would treasure that moment for the rest of her life.

Perhaps it was her rapturous thoughts as she got off the bus at home that kept Lydia from noticing the strange, expensive car parked in the shade of the ancient oak trees in her yard, for she glided by without noticing it, and when she stepped inside the front door, Lydia was shocked to see not one stranger, but two sitting on her living room sofa. One of the strangers looked up at her and smiled with lips covered in lipstick and batted her eyes with mascara laden lashes. She wore a chiffon dress with a matching flowery hat and glossy high heeled shoes.

"Why, hello, my dear." She stood up to greet Lydia, holding out her hand to shake Lydia's, but Lydia did not know what to do and just stood there staring at her with her mouth gaping open.

"Lydia, have some manners," said the other stranger with an air of authority. "This is Miss Loraine, and she has come with some wonderful news for me," the stranger smiled and looked at Miss Loraine with the utmost admiration.

"Mom?" Lydia eked out the title, "You're out?"

Chappell blushed deeply.

"Of course I'm out, Lydia, don't be foolish. Now shake hands with Miss Loraine like someone who has been raised right," Chappell gushed.

Lydia weakly shook Miss Loraine's hand.

"Actually, I was just leaving, but it is a pleasure to have met you, Lydia, before I had to leave. I was praying for just such an opportunity."

"Yes, ma'am," Lydia replied, still a bit dazed at seeing her mother out of her room. She kept staring at her mother until Chappell, unnerved, stood up and took Miss Loraine by the arm to usher her to the door.

"You'll come back soon?" Chappell asked earnestly.

"Oh, yes, my dear. I never leave a convert unattended to take on this world by herself. We will study the Bible together each week, so be sure and read the passages that I assigned you today, alright? Lydia, it was a real pleasure to meet you. Perhaps you can join us in our study of the Bible. Take care, now."

"Bye, Miss Loraine, take care," Chappell closed the door and then turned to go to her room.

"Mom, wait. Where're ya' goin'? Who was that, and what did she mean when she called ya' a convert? You're out--out here. When? Why? What's happened?"

"Lydia, ya' make me feel so foolish with yer questions. I'm going to lie down now, so please don't bother me agin' with questions," Chappell walked quickly away to the back porch bedroom, clutching her new Bible to her chest. A few moments later, Lydia heard her mother's door slam.

Wait until Darius hears about this, she thought. Lydia went about her chores, but was sorely distracted and found herself doing many simple tasks over again because she could not focus. Thoughts about David and her mother warred for dominance in her mind, and she could not find rest in her emotions from either one of them. Finally, at bedtime, when she was actually in her bed under the covers, Lydia let the thoughts about her mother go and fostered her images of David and the enchanted lunch, and on these thoughts she drifted to sleep.

Darius woke Lydia a little after midnight, frightening her out of her wits. She jumped up and grabbed his sleeve.

"What's wrong? Are ya' alright?" she asked.

"Yeah, but somethin' else is wrong. Listen!" he whispered.

They both sat motionless on the side of Lydia's bed, taking in the total silence around them, a silence broken only by the stroking of cricket legs and the low bellowing of bull frogs.

"Ya' see? She ain't come out to yell at Dad tonight. Ya' think she's dead, or sick, or somethin'? Should we go knock on her door and find out?" Darius asked with a tremor in his voice.

"I don't think so, Darius," Lydia answered and proceeded to tell Darius about Miss Loraine and about Chappell being out in the living room that afternoon.

"Miss Loraine called her a convert, and gave her a Bible, so maybe that's why she ain't yelling tonight, 'cause converts can't do that kind of thing."

"Man, I can't sleep without that noise," Darius said, and they both laughed quietly.

"Well, go back and try, and don't scare me like that again," Lydia scolded, pushing him off her bed. Darius went back to his bed but remained awake wondering what it meant to be a convert while Lydia closed her eyes and allowed thoughts about David to lull her back to sleep.

The rest of that semester was spent having lunch with David which in turn changed her status with her peers. No longer was she harassed in the hallway or teased in class, and if there was whispering, it didn't bother her because she knew it was about her and David, a young man most of the girls in class would have given their eye teeth to be with. Though they only saw each other at school, Lydia and David were able to build a relationship very much like that of a dating couple, and one day David asked her to go out with him. It was a mild day in May, and they had moved under the shade of one of the ornamental trees in the atrium and were holding hands.

"How about it, Lydia, go out with me?" David leaned over close enough to kiss her.

"I told ya', I can't," she said and pushed him back playfully.

"Yeah, but you never tell me why. I'm beginning to think you don't like me."

"That's it, David. That's why I eat lunch with ya' everyday and see ya' between almost every class."

"I have an idea. Let's get off the bus at Woolworth's and hang out after school, then I can give you a ride back to your house later when my old man picks me up. What do you say?" David asked kissing the back of her hand.

Lydia smiled. The idea was wonderful to her, but impossible. Her father would kill her, and though it was her plan to die anyway, she would rather do it her own way.

"Look, David, I think the world of ya', but you and I both know that when the summer hits, I won't see ya' agin', and when the school year starts next year, you'll pro'bly be with somebody new. So let's not complicate this, okay? Let's just be friends. We both know that I don't belong in yer world."

"Wish you wouldn't say that all the time" David replied. "It makes me sound like a snob, and I'm not a snob, you know."

Lydia stuck to her conviction and never went out on a date of any kind with David, though she desperately wanted to see him away from school. There was always a strong voice of caution compelling her not to let her guard down, that this was all make believe and would certainly end soon, so she held out to the end of school when a strange thing happened that would change the course of her life and David's.

Since that afternoon when Miss Loraine had visited their home, Chappell had been in the kitchen every afternoon when Lydia came home from school. She was always reading her Bible, but shortly after Lydia would enter the room, Chappell would pack away her Bible and the notes she had taken and move back to the solitary confinement of her bedroom off the porch where she would stay until the next day. She never came out at night anymore to rage at Earl, and she had taken to smiling at Lydia when she saw her.

One day, Chappell did not leave when Lydia came into the kitchen. She stayed at the table reading and writing her notes. Lydia went about her chores, lighting a fire in the stove for cooking, taking out vegetables that she had prepared the night before, boiling water, frying meat, bringing in firewood, and setting the table for the supper meal. As Lydia was putting plates around the table, she stopped and glared at Chappell until she looked up.

"Am I in yer way?" Chappell asked and began to gather her Bible and notes to leave the table.

"In my way? How can ya' be in my way, Mom? I'm in yer way here. I'm doin' all the things that you should be doin', that you should have been doin' all these years so I could live a normal life, and so my own father and brother wouldn't hate my guts. Yes, you're in my way! I hate seeing ya' out here! I hate seeing ya' all of a sudden living a life that ya' want to live, when I can't live the life I want to live! What right do ya' have to be smilin' and happy? What right do ya' have to sit in that dingy little room, with people waitin' on ya' hand and foot, when I can't go sit in my room and read because I have to do all the grownup things that you refused to do for so long? I hate ya'! You hear me? I hate ya', and I don't care if you're converted, or if you read that Bible all day, I still hate ya' for what ya' did to my life!"

Chappell had started to slowly creep away, holding her Bible and notes close to her chest, trying to get out of the kitchen and into her haven before anything terrible happened. She didn't have the nerve to look at Lydia while she was railing at her, and it hurt her heart to be treated in such a way by her own daughter. Chappell was humiliated, and finally reaching her door, turned to Lydia to say something strong, but couldn't bring herself to do it.

"I love ya', Lydia, and Darius, too," she feebly spoke, and quickly retreated to her room.

Lydia stood there aghast. Had she really spoken those horrific words to her own mother? What kind of animal had she become to be able to hurt someone that way? Lydia sat in the straw bottomed chair next to the stove and buried her head in her hands and cried. Oh, God, she thought, if you're really out there, forgive me, and let me make it up to her somehow.

It wasn't long before her prayer was answered. The following day, as Lydia came into the front door after school, she was met by the lady with the impeccable make up and beautiful clothes, Miss Loraine. The gracious lady stood up and met Lydia at the door, taking Lydia by the hand and bidding her to sit beside the gentile lady on the sofa.

"Your mother and I have been talking about you, Lydia, but it was good talk. She's very proud of her children and wants only the best for them, so she has agreed to allow you to come to our church camp this summer, in the month of June. The camp is for high school students only and is located at Apache Cave here in Virginia. There is a lake, horse shoes, caves for exploring, and a snack shop. You are going to love it, Lydia." the sweet lady beamed.

Lydia looked at Chappell who looked back at her with such pleading in her eyes that Lydia could not resist. It would be a way to pay her mother back for all the harsh words she had flung at her, and it would also be a time to be away from her father for awhile. Besides, she could use the time to plan for her suicide and write a letter to Darius about it all so he would not feel so badly.

"How would I get there?"

"I will pick you up myself and we'll go to my church where we'll meet the other teens who will be riding the bus with you. Oh, Lydia, I am so excited about you going. You're really going to love it."

Miss Loraine was hugging Lydia but holding hands with her mother behind her back, winking at Chappell and giving her the okay sign. Apparently, Chappell had asked Miss Loraine to handle talking Lydia into going. It had worked, but only because of Lydia's guilt.

The school year came to an end with the whole family, even Chappell, and including Miss Loraine, attending Darius's graduation outside on the football field of the high school. Lydia was so proud of Darius who got a scholarship from the state university to play basketball for them in the fall, but she felt such a pain of regret that he would not be at school with her next year, or living at home with her anymore. He was leaving in a week to go live in the dorm in Richmond and get a summer job to make some spare money for school. She cried both tears of joy and tears of grief as she hugged her brother after the ceremony. Nobody could ever take his place in her heart. Nobody.

Chapter Eight

Chappell had begun getting up before the rest of the family in the mornings and had breakfast cooked by the time Lydia got dressed. At first, this irritated Lydia because she was so ingrained in her schedule that she didn't know what to do with all the extra time, and she hated the feeling that her mother was only trying to show off somehow because she was supposed to be converted some sort of way, but soon Lydia learned how to use the mornings to catch up on school work and reading so that the mornings became an enjoyable time for her. Earl took to sitting beside the stove talking to Chappell as she cooked, watching her move about in the kitchen, and smiling at her when she wasn't looking. It certainly took his mind off Lydia, and she went about the home unnoticed and uncriticized for a change. Could life really have taken a turn for the better?

It was very warm and sunny the morning that Miss Loraine showed up to fetch Lydia for camp. Since Darius had left for Richmond, Lydia was very lonely and so didn't mind the thought of leaving for camp as much as she thought she would. Though Chappell was helping around the house more now, Lydia and she still did not have a good rapport, and the tenseness caused Chappell to flee to her room off the porch as soon as a chore was done, leaving Lydia alone again.

"Good morning, Lydia! I hope you are as excited as I am this morning!" beamed Miss Loraine.

"Yes, ma'am," Lydia replied politely.

"Well, let me go and speak with your mama, and then we'll be off. You can put your…uh…bag in the back seat of my car, okay?"

"Yes, ma'am," Lydia said obediently and headed to the car with her gunnysack of belongings.

Miss Loraine was only in the house a few minutes before she and Chappell both came out onto the front porch. Chappell came down the porch steps to Lydia, tentatively holding up her arms as if to ask for a hug. Lydia was torn. She didn't really want her mother touching her right now, but also didn't want to add to her crimes against God by embarrassing her mother in front of the person who was probably Chappell's only friend, so Lydia leaned forward and gingerly hugged her mother.

"Oh, thank ya', Lydia! I do love ya'," her mother crooned as she held Lydia for a long moment.

"Well, it's time! Toodle-loo, Chappell. I hope you have a great week! Bi, now!"

Lydia sat on the soft leather seat of Miss Loraine's car and left for the church where she met about a hundred other campers from other churches in the local area who were all headed to this same camp. It's going to be a long week, Lydia thought as she climbed into the huge charter bus and sat next to another girl who apparently did not know anybody else either.

"Hi, I'm Angel," she said holding out her hand to Lydia.

"You're kiddin', right?" Lydia asked incredulously.

The girl laughed, "No, that's really my name. I think my parents were a bit high at the time, but nevertheless, that's what I go by. What's yours?"

"Lydia," she said and shook the girl's hand.

"It's nice to meet you, Lydia. Do you know who your cabin mates are yet?"

"What's a cabin mate?"

Angel laughed again, "You know, the people in your cabin. There are eight girls in each cabin. So do you know who your cabin mates are yet?"

"I guess not. How do I find out?" Lydia asked reluctantly.

"Well, you could ask Miss Loraine before we pull out. Go on, I'll save your seat."

Lydia milled through the crowds in and out between the buses until she came across Miss Loraine who told her that she was in cabin number 3, but that she did not know who all the other girls were right off the bat. Armed with this knowledge, Lydia headed back to her bus and sat down beside her new friend.

"I'm in cabin number three," she reported.

Angel gasped, "So am I! That's so cool! At this point, you are the only person I know, and I don't even really know you yet, but I'm glad you're in my cabin."

Lydia smiled at her. She seemed safe enough, and it was good to be able have someone with which to hang out right at the start. Maybe this would not be such a bad week after all.

The camp ground was small and quaint with activities located at strategic points on the grounds, and a large, covered, chapel type structure right in the middle of everything. All the campers were herded into the large chapel, registered by cabins, and given their study aids to go along with the Bible studies they would do each day. Lydia and Angel went to cabin number three and met the other girls, all of whom seemed nice enough to Lydia, but around whom Lydia felt strange and out of place as if they belonged to a certain club of which she was unaware, like some of the clubs at her high school that most students never knew existed until the yearbook came out in the spring, and the elite members were pictured in their evening gowns and tuxedos. Nevertheless, she smiled at her fellow campers and spoke only when she was spoken to, being sure to use her best pronunciations and finish her words lest they sense that she was just a country girl after all and not worthy of their kindness.

Everyone had her own Bible, and Lydia wished that she had brought the Bible her mother was using, but Chappell probably would not have let it out of her sight. Angel shared her Bible with

Lydia for most parts of the study, but there were times when the girls were supposed to separate and study alone which left Lydia without any means of information from which to answer the questions in her study guide, and this made her feel stupid and unlearned. She would listen intently, however, to the lessons being taught and take in every word so that she could use it to answer the questions even though she had no Bible in front of her. Fortunately, the counselor who was teaching the lessons would not call on anyone who did not want to answer, so Lydia felt safe in the group and could relax and listen. Most of what she heard made no real sense to her, though, and she began to wonder what all the hoopla was about.

Each night, after a rather long and boring sermon given by the man who was head of the camp, Mr. Landon, many of the teens would go forward, fall on their knees at the bench-looking altar, and cry until an adult counselor came and got them, sitting with them on the front row, asking them questions, and finally, praying with them to be saved. Afterwards, each one would stand in front of the crowd and tell what a bad sinner they had become in their short lives, but what a miracle had happened now that they were saved by God through Jesus.

Lydia felt angry at this display. How can God just let these people go after some of the things they say they did and not hold them accountable, like her mother, who ruined Lydia's life, but because she was now saved, everything was alright, and Lydia was supposed to forget it ever happened and be happy that her mother had a life again? No way, Lydia decided. If this is what God is about, I don't want any part of it, and she left the meeting before it was over and went to her cabin to think about all these things.

Wednesday, the middle of the camp week, was a particularly hot, sultry day and most of the kids were seeking out the deepest shade in which to study their lessons. Lydia and Angel sat directly in front of Angel's rotating fan in the shade of the cabin and read their Bibles and answered the questions for the after lunch session.

"I think it's about time for lunch now, Lydia. Let's go get a place in line," Angel said wiping her brow with a tissue.

"I may skip lunch today and stand in a cold shower instead," Lydia answered.

"Then there won't be any water left in the well for the rest of us later, you know," Angel pointed out to her.

"You're right. Let's go to lunch," Lydia acquiesced and got her towel to wipe off her face, arms, and neck. "Man, I can't believe it's so hot!"

The girls stood in line at the entrance of the cafeteria with the others who could not stand the heat any longer until Mr. Landon let them inside early just so they could get out of the sun and into the shade of the open cafeteria. A little later, a hot dog lunch was served with lots of water and juice to drink, and Lydia and Angel finally felt a little relief from the heat. Mr. Landon stood up near the end of the meal to make a special announcement.

"May I have your attention, please, and could everyone look this way for a minute?" he asked while banging on the bottom of a metal pan with a wooden spoon. The room grew hushed. "I would like to invite anyone who is interested to join me outside here at the campfire area for a special prayer meeting right after lunch. I know it will take away your recreation time, but I believe it will be far more valuable to you than horse shoes or swimming. Anyone who is interested can join me at the campfire area right after we dismiss from lunch."

"Do you want to go to this prayer meeting?" Angel asked Lydia.

"I don't think so. I don't really do that kind of stuff," Lydia replied.

"Well, I think I'm going, so I'll see you later," Angel smiled and gave Lydia a quick hug before leaving to throw away her paper plate and trash.

Lydia watched Angel leave the cafeteria and then sat there looking around at the other campers, none of whom she had really gotten to know that week as well as she knew Angel. Maybe she could go back and sleep in front of the fan during recreation time? The longer Lydia sat there alone, the more out of place she felt until finally she jumped up, threw away her plate and trash, and stepped outside the screened lunch room to find Angel.

A small group of four girls and one guy were gathered together at the campfire site which was next to the Chapel building.

All around them, a hundred other campers were talking, screaming at the pool, clanking horse shoes, yelling at each other from their canoes on the large pond, or laughing at each other as they played board games in the shade. Lydia felt like an idiot approaching the small group, but she joined them, sitting on the end of a thick log that was the seating around the campfire site, and waited for the little prayer session to begin.

"Glad you could join us, Lydia," genuinely greeted Mr. Landon. Lydia feebly smiled and looked at Angel who was beaming that Lydia had joined them for prayer. This is crazy, thought Lydia, I can't even hear myself think, much less pray, so how's God going to hear anything?

"Young people, before we begin to pray, I would like to tell you all something about God and about his son, Jesus. You see, we are all born with sinful natures, and that's why it is so easy for us to sin as we grow older until the next thing you know, we don't even recognize our actions as sinful. We are separated from God by our sins, and He does not want us to be separated from Him because, like any loving father, He wants us to be close to Him and to fellowship with Him because He loves us so much. God our Creator and our Father loves us so much and desires so much to draw us back to Him, and into His family, and into His care and loving arms, that He asked His only son, Jesus, to sacrifice Himself for us all to cleanse us from our sins, so that we could once again be in the presence of God, our Father."

Lydia suddenly felt mesmerized by what this man was saying. She had been without the love of a father for so long that this message seized her heart and she yearned to know more. Could she actually have a father who loved and cared for her, and who would be with her all the time? Was this really possible?

Mr. Landon continued, "God says in the book of the Apostle John, chapter one, verse twelve, that as many as received Him [meaning Jesus Christ, the son of God], to them God gives the right to become the children of God, even to those who believe in His name. Let's pray."

As every one bowed their heads, and Mr. Landon began to pray out loud, Lydia also bowed her head. God, I want that, she said in her spirit. Suddenly, she heard a mighty rushing wind so strong that it drowned out the noise of campers playing. Lydia looked up to see if a storm had blown in, but all was still and hot, and the praying camper's hair was still stuck to the sides of their faces from the humidity, and Mr. Landon was still droning on in his prayer. She closed her eyes again, and there was the mighty rushing wind, and in the midst of the wind, she saw a face, and he said, "You are mine!" Lydia gasped out loud, opening her eyes, realizing that she had just met Jesus. How she knew it was Jesus was a mystery to her, but she was certain that that was who it was, and He had told her that she was His, that she belonged to God now. She had a Father, and this Father loved her completely and would be in her forever!

Lydia jumped up and grabbed Mr. Landon by the arm while he was still praying out loud, and cried, "I've met Him! I've met Jesus!" She then turned to her puzzled friend, and grabbing her by the arms said, "I know Him, and He said that I'm His! What do I do now?"

Angel hugged her strange friend, and together they left the campsite, rejoicing in spirit, singing any of the camp songs they knew by heart that seemed to fit the occasion. Lydia was elated like someone who had been asleep all her life, but was suddenly and miraculously awakened. Everything seemed new to her. She could hear all of nature around her harmoniously praising God for their very existence. All Lydia wanted to do was read a Bible, so she confiscated Angel's Bible for the rest of the day and read it through supper that night until it was time for the chapel service.

It was all she could do to sit still during the service that night. Lydia sang out the Christian choruses for the first time that week in a voice so strong and melodious that it not only surprised her, but caught the notice of everyone else around her, too. The sermon made sense to Lydia that night, and she saw for the first time the real compassion that Mr. Landon had for his campers, and she understood the urgency of his message to them. It made her love and appreciate him, feelings that she had never had for any one before. Finally, the sermon came to an end and the invitation to come forward to be saved was given. Lydia hastily climbed over the campers on her bench to go forward, but she did not stop at the altar, rather she searched the front row for an adult counselor who could tell her what to do now that she was a child of God. Lydia grabbed a lady named Ester.

"Can you help me?" Lydia pleaded with tears in her eyes.

"Of course I can help you, dear," replied Ester, misinterpreting Lydia's tears. "Shall we pray the sinner's prayer together?"

"No, ma'am, you see, I'm saved already. I met Jesus this afternoon at the prayer meeting. I just want to know what I do now. What does God want me to do now?"

Ester began to flip through her counselor notes searching for the right procedure to handle such a request, but could not find a pat response.

"Let's see, honey, I don't know quite what to tell you. I guess you just begin to read your Bible and pray everyday, and God Himself will show you the rest."

Lydia thanked the lady and then went back to her seat a little disappointed that there was not something set in writing that would guide her in knowing Jesus a little better. Then a small quiet voice said, "You have the Bible." Lydia looked around to see who might have spoken to her, but everyone's heads were bowed. God, is that you, she asked silently? Maybe that's how he would keep in touch with her, through the Bible. She lowered her head and began to talk to her new Father.

"God, do I call you God? Some people here call you Lord, so do I call you God? And Jesus, are you there, too? What was the wind, does it have a name? Is all this real? How can I know if all this is real, or if I'm just losing my mind? Help me to know, please," Lydia prayed, and knelt at her bench waiting for an answer. After a few minutes, she felt a presence there with her, not in the flesh, but in her spirit, and it was so comforting and warm that she knew it was real. This presence filled her with contentment like she had never known before and instilled in her courage to face anything. Lydia knew that her life from now on would be truly different, that she would walk in a different realm.

The rest of the camp week, Lydia babbled on and on about God and all that she read about him each day until even Angel told her to back off a little, that there were other things to talk about, but Angel had not been brought back to life like Lydia, and to Lydia there was nothing else in the world worth talking about more than her Lord and Savior. She was alive again for the first time since she was nine years old, and she could remember the reason for the bright sunshine. There would be nothing and nobody who could frighten her now, for her Father would always be with her and protect her and show her what to do in every situation. Lydia could talk about nothing else.

On the last day of camp, after all the cabins had been cleaned, and all the campers had packed, Lydia walked by a trash can full of cast away items, and there on top of a heap of trash lay a

Bible, though one would not have known right away that it was a Bible, for the first dozen chapters of Genesis and the last couple of chapters of Revelation had been torn away along with the cover. Nevertheless, Lydia recognized what it was and snatched it out of the trash, clutching it close to her heart, and thanking Jesus for it all the way to the bus. She had her own Bible at last!

Chapter Nine

Lydia grabbed her pitiful gunny sack of clothes out of Miss Loraine's car trunk, hugged her goodbye, and headed up the back steps into the screened porch forgetting that is was a Sunday and that her father would be home. She bounced into the kitchen smiling and humming the tune from one of the choruses she had learned at camp, unaware that her mother was sitting at the table with her Bible. About the time Lydia looked up and saw Chappell, Earl came into the room with a scowl on his face, and Lydia instinctively looked away to lessen the inevitable confrontation.

"Whadda" ya" mean crashin' into the house that way when yer mom is tryin' to read? Git to yer room and git ready to catch up on some of these chores 'round here that piled up while you were gone," he ordered strolling over to sit down at the table across from Chappell.

"Whatcha' readin' this time?" he asked jerking his head toward the open Bible.

"The book of Mark," she replied, "and you didn't have to be so hard on Lydia. She just got home a secon' ago." Chappell got up and started gathering her study notes and Bible together.

"Where're ya' goin'? Sit down. Lydia can handle suppa'. You read," Earl commanded and got up to leave.

"Since when do ya' orda' me around?" Chappell glared at him, and then left to go to the bedroom off the kitchen, Earl's room.

When did she start living there, Lydia mused as she began to stoke the fire? Earl stomped out of the room, and Lydia gave a sigh of relief while striking the long match to start a fire in the large black cook stove. Why wasn't Chappell doing this, she wondered? She seemed to be herself again, and she had even moved back into the bedroom with Earl, so why was Lydia fixing supper when her mother could have already had it done by the time Lydia got home. Lydia began to feel familiar old emotions creeping into her heart, and she poked harder than necessary at the dry hickory logs trying to arrange them so they would ignite more quickly. This isn't right. God lived in her now, so how could she still feel this anger and hatred for another person, especially her mother? Had God left her now? Was she too ugly and horrible after all for Him to stay with her?

Lydia could not stop the hot tears that began to pour over her cheeks and run scalding down her face. She had failed God, and now He no longer wanted her. She could not feel Him with her, so He must have left. Lydia shook with sobs and sat down on the rickety ladder backed chair behind the wood stove, feeling more dejected and sorrowful than she had ever felt in her entire life. No, no, no, God would not do that to her, not the God she had learned about at camp. He said that she was His, and Lydia just knew that it was true.

"Oh, Jesus, if you'll give me anotha' chance, I'll do betta', but this hate runs so deep and hurts so bad, can ya' eva' help me lose it? Please help me, and please don't go away! I love ya' so much, and I want to trust ya'," Lydia prayed with her head in her apron, weeping quietly so her father would not hear and come into the room to scold her. Getting up to adjust the damper on the stove pipe and the baffles on the front of the big iron stove, Lydia felt hopeful. God could do this. He could make her into a decent person--someone likeable, and smart, and beautiful—and she could really be His child.

That night, after Earl and Chappell had retired to their bedroom, Lydia tiptoed out to the kitchen and confiscated the kerosene lantern, the one reserved for kitchen use only, and sneaked back to her room with it as there was no lantern reserved for her room. Bedtime would probably be the only time available for her to study her Bible since there were so many household chores awaiting her each morning, and with the vegetable gardens coming in, she could add canning to the seemingly interminable list of work.

Lydia closed her bedroom door as quietly as possible, and sitting on her bed with her unusual Bible, she situated the lantern on the wide windowsill of her open window, lit the kerosene-soaked wick of the lantern, and started reading where her Bible began, chapter 14 of Genesis where someone named Abraham rescued someone named Lot and gave tithe money to someone named Melchizadek. It was all very interesting and historical, and Lydia liked to read history, but the confusion over who these people were and the significance of it all was overwhelming, and Lydia became discouraged. How would she ever understand the Bible if she could not start from the beginning?

Sighing, Lydia began to flip through the pages of her Bible, reading a little here and there in the Old Testament, and becoming very interested in the events of which she was reading, realizing that the whole Bible was an account of God's dealings with mankind, like a diary almost, and that if she continued to read, she would begin to understand some of what she had missed. Excited by this prospect, Lydia began once more in Genesis chapter 14, only this time she had her pencil and notebook ready to take notes and keep up with what she had read so she could compare it with later events.

She was not sure how much time had elapsed when Earl slammed her door against the wall, causing her sleepy eyes to fly open in surprise. He had never come into her room before, much less in such a rage, and she crouched on the bed next to the open window, slowly moving the lit lamp out of the way, ready to leap outside to the ground if necessary.

"What in hell do ya' think you're doin'? Wastin' good oil, and for what? Who told ya' you could take that lantern outa' the kitchen? Huh!? Answer me! What are ya' doin' in here anyway at this hour of the night that warrants ya' usin' up the kitchen lantern oil?" he seethed.

"I was readin'," Lydia answered shakily, instinctively lowering her gaze in an attempt to ward off any repercussions from her father's anger. Slowly she uncurled her legs from under her and slithered to a stand next to her bed, reaching for the lamp in the window. "I'll put it back right now, Dad. I was just tryin' to read my Bible," she attempted explaining.

"Yer what? Let me see that thing," Earl grabbed the Bible out of Lydia's hand and held it close to his face, apparently trying to make out the small print. He then flipped through the pages carelessly and laughed out loud. "How do ya' know this here's a Bible? It's missin' half its pages. But it don't matter none if it's a Bible or not, I don't want ya' sneakin' my kitchen lantern and using my expensive oil for yer night time pleasures. Besides, it ain't natr'al for a youngster to want to read the Bible, and ya' need yer sleep for doing yer chores in the mornin', so git to bed, and don't let me catch ya' doin' this agin', ya' hear?" he jerked the lantern out of Lydia's other hand.

"But Dad, when else can I read? What's so bad about wantin' to…?"

"Don't back talk me! What right do ya' have to be beggin' me 'bout this?"

"But, but Mom and you are back…I mean, she's in yer room, and I thought…"

"Ya' thought what?" Earl drawled the words out like a challenge, leaning toward Lydia in a particularly threatening manner.

Lydia looked down, but kept going with her argument, "Now that Mom is back to bein' part of the family, I thought you'd be happy…that you'd not be so mad at me all the time."

Earl's tawdry contemptuous laugh made Lydia blush.

"Why should I be happy 'bout that? Just 'cause she's outta' that room don't mean she's back to bein' part of the family, not really," Earl leaned closer to Lydia's face, but she was looking down and turned her face away from him so she could not see the contempt in his eyes that she heard in his voice. "She still blames me for what happened to you, to us, to everybody in this whole family! Now, genius, tell me agin' why that should make me happy."

Something Earl said in that moment so distracted Lydia from the fearful confrontation that she forgot who she was. Feeling a surge of power and courage, the cowering girl straightened up, looked her father square in the eyes, and asked him point blank, "What did happen to me?"

Earl blinked hard and backed away from Lydia. This was the first time he had seen Lydia's eyes since she was nine years old, and he was taken back by the sight of those beautiful green eyes looking straight into his face, straight into his soul. There was something unspeakable in her gaze: strength he had never known existed, strength not of cheap intimidation, but of real authority and command. At that moment, Earl knew he had lost his reign over Lydia, and he drew up his shoulders and turned away from her towards the door, but before he could leave, she asked him the question again.

"What did happen to me?" Lydia grabbed his arm, but he flung her hand away with a twist of his elbow and whirled around.

"You don't remember?" He asked her with the same confused twist of his eyebrows that she had seen years ago while standing in his bedroom among the broken shards of a glass bottle. Lydia could almost smell the whiskey as she recalled that moment.

"I only remember wakin' up in the small bedroom off the back porch," she answered him.

He took in a deep breath, heaving his chest upwards, and said, looking down his nose at her. "Well, it's pro'bly best," and turned to walk away.

"No, it's not best for me!" Lydia cried out after him.

Earl stopped and spoke sternly to her without turning around, "I promised yer mom we'd never speak of it agin', and I ain't breakin' that promise!" He continued to his room, leaving the kerosene lantern on the antique hutch as he passed by, and tossing Lydia's Bible into the wood chip box to be used as kindling for the cook stove fires.

Lydia stood there in a puddle of moonlight in the middle of her bedroom floor. She felt emotions so strong that her chest ached and her clenched jaws cringed from the tension. It was not a dream. Something had happened to her after all. More than ever Lydia wished her brother, Darius, was there. Perhaps he could tell her something about that incident that would cause her to remember. It did not occur to Lydia at that time to pray for memory, but she did realize that God had given her unique courage that night, and that in a small arena, she had won a victory over her father's intimidation, and for this reason, Lydia knelt for a while in the glowing moonlight and praised God in hushed phrases and with muffled tears of joy. She then stole softly into the kitchen, to the wood chip box, and reclaimed her Bible. Bible reading would have to be done by moonlight until the end of the summer, then she could take the Bible with her to school and read it at lunch in her secret nook, but until then Lydia would have to find a safe hiding place for it during the day, or her father would destroy it.

She was tucking it under her mattress when Lydia remembered the small brown bag in which she had put her pitifully chopped off locks of hair many years ago and which had disappeared mysteriously from this particular hiding place, so she retrieved the Bible from under the mattress and searched the sparsely furnished bedroom for another hiding place. Darius' bed was sitting there unused and made up nicely. Perhaps no one would think to look under his mattress. Better yet, maybe she could slit the threads at the corner, and slide the Bible just beneath the ticking cover on the underside where it would not be seen even if the mattress was lifted. This seemed good to Lydia, and so using her teeth, she sawed through a few threads and slipped her treasured Bible inside its new hideaway. Now she could sleep in peace.

The rest of the summer, Lydia stealthily read and studied her Bible, using the bright moonbeams as light with which to see, and as she read, the eager girl learned more and more about the God who had saved her, and as her confidence in God grew, Lydia's altercations with Earl also grew until one day, Chappell took Lydia aside to talk with her. They sat on the plump feather-filled bed in Chappell's room facing each other, both nervously looking around until finally Lydia spoke up.

"What did ya' wanta' talk about?"

"Oh, well, just this thing with you an yer dad. He loves ya', Lydia. He has to, he's yer father, but it's just that you can see right through 'im, and that makes him very uncomfortable."

"No, I can't."

"Yes, Lydia, ya' can. You're special, Lydia, you've always been. There's always been somethin' 'bout ya' that was, well, differnt. Now that you've gone and got saved, well, yer dad, he feels like ya' look down on him, but I know it's not that, Lydia. Ya' just have a powa' in ya' now that yer dad can't take away, and he can't make ya' fear him no more, that's why he fights ya' so," Chappell looked down at her lap before continuing.

"I want ya' to promise me somethin', Lydia," her mother pleaded. "I want ya' to pray for yer father. He just needs to be saved, ya' know. Can ya' promise me that?"

Lydia regarded her mother with a frown on her face. Chappell seemed to her to be a weak person, bound by fear, and though she was now helping Lydia a little in the mornings with breakfast, Lydia still resented her mother thrusting all the rest of her normal household duties onto Lydia. She had come to disrespect her mother and avoided her as much as possible because she couldn't handle the feelings of anger that welled up inside of her when her mother was around. Now here was Chappell actually asking favors of Lydia as if she wasn't already asking too much of her.

"I don't know, Mom. He's yer husband, not mine, and I already feel like I'm doin' too much of yer duties as it is."

Chappell looked down at the bed again, "I know ya' are. I don't know why I can't bring myself to help ya'. I just know that there's more out there in this world, and to be stuck in this drudgery is so hard…"

"Tell me about it! It's been so hard for me for the last 8 years! See these scars?" Lydia stood up and held out her arms so her mother could see the burn marks from her attempts at cooking when she was so little, "and rememba' my hair? And who do ya' think got the privilege of emptyin' yer potty all these years? See the ends of my fingers? The FBI wouldn't recognize me by my fingerprints if they had to!" Lydia was steaming mad. "The thing that bugs me most is that I can't even be the person I know God wants me to be 'cause I can't stop hatin' you long enough," Lydia sat back down on the edge of the billowy bed crying and defeated.

Chappell did not know what to say. All these years she had so intently focused blame on Earl for Lydia's ruin that her own culpability in her daughter's emotional blight had escaped her. She was somewhat shocked and could not speak. Reaching out her hand, Chappell touched Lydia's shoulder.

"I have somethin' to show ya'," she said timidly, and proceeded to get off the high bed and scurry over to a ancient oak dresser where she took the very bottom drawer completely out and reached far back to the dresser frame pulling out a small, crinkled, brown sandwich bag folded over several times to keep the contents from spilling out. Gazing at it lovingly, Chappell walked slowly back to the bed and held out the crumpled old bag to Lydia who stared at it in disbelief for a moment before taking it from her hand.

"You…why?" she asked still staring at the little bag. She felt weak and wanted to lie down in her own room. It was all too much, too tense, too surreal.

"It was all I had of ya'. It was all I could touch of ya' at the time 'cause of all that had happened. You will neva' know how much havin' that piece of ya' meant to me or how much it helped me hang on here when I thought…"Chappell looked down at the floor as tears spilled over her cheeks and ran down her sad face, "…when I thought this family was foreva' destroyed."

Lydia was straining to hold back her tears. To cry in front of this woman would be unthinkable; it would make her as weak as her mother. Yet, here was her hair, and there was her mother telling her that she did care enough to steal it away--probably so Earl could not find it--and keep it for her until now to show her how much she loved her. Lydia's wall of resistance was crumbling.

"I gotta' think about all this," she said, and departed quickly from the room, closing the door behind her so Chappell could not follow. In her room, Lydia sat on her bed and opened the treasured bag, pulling out the long dark locks of hair, and then it was all over. Years of anguish poured out of her in the form of loud wails, torrents of tears, and a racked her weary body. She could not stop the aching in her heart, and for what seemed like hours, Lydia unleashed her passionate grief, beating the bed with her fists, falling to the floor on her knees in groaning prayers for which she had no words, only fervent emotion. She remained in this state until dusk, at which time her energy was depleted, and she lay curled up on her side gazing out the window at the tops of the swaying trees, watching the sun sink in the sky. Earl would be home from work soon and expect to see his supper on the table, so Lydia feebly arose to go about her duties, but when she opened her bedroom door the aroma of mashed potatoes, gravy, green beans, baked biscuits, and fried chicken reached her nostrils, and she stopped in her tired tracks and blinked in disbelief.

"I thought ya' could use a rest," Chappell said pointing to the table, "so I fixed suppa' tonight. Come on now, and you can eat 'fore yer dad gets home." Chappell spooned food onto a plate as she spoke and handed the meal to Lydia.

"Thank ya', but if ya' don't mind, I'll eat in my room tonight, okay?"

"Whateva' ya' want," Chappell smiled genuinely at Lydia.

Lydia stayed in her room the rest of the night eating and then sleeping until dawn when she once again heard the noises of someone moving about in the kitchen starting a fire and getting ready to cook. God really did love her, didn't He? He loved them all, the whole crazy bizarre lot of them. Lydia realized for the first time that she was not the only one in the family in need of healing, and she agreed in her heart to pray with her mother for her father's salvation, and for Darius' salvation, too. For the first time since she had met Jesus, Lydia felt a type of calling, a calling to pray. It gave her a very strong reason to get out of bed in the morning and face the bright shining sun whose presence was becoming dear to Lydia for the first time since she was nine years old.

Chapter Ten

The rest of that summer passed, as Lydia prayed, rather uneventfully with Lydia and her mother working together on the chores, and Chappell refusing to allow Earl to farm Lydia out to strangers that year. They'd make up the money somehow, she had said, and she needed Lydia there to help her for a change, so Earl acquiesced and seemed almost relieved to see his wife with some companionship since she did not yet appear to want his to a large degree. They were sleeping together, but were as yet not acting as husband and wife; nevertheless he loved Chappell beyond any other feeling he had ever known, and was willing to continue waiting as long as it took for her to love him again.

About the middle of August, as the family was sitting on the front porch with Earl picking softly at his guitar, and Lydia and Chappell snapping green beans into bowls, a strange car rolled down the long dirt drive toward the house. Everyone ceased what they were doing and with furrowed brow—as company was not a common occurrence at this home—watched the car work its way carefully over the rutted drive and come to a stop in the shade of the sprawling oak trees in the side yard. The family had risen and was standing at the end of the front porch wondering who this might be when the door on the driver's side swung opened, and out stepped Darius

"Hi, ya'll!" he yelled as he walked around the end of the car and headed toward the porch.

"Darius! Oh, my goodness!" Lydia cried out, and placing her hand on the edge of the porch, leaped to the ground and ran toward him, throwing her arms around his neck as he grabbed her about her waist and swung her full circle before setting her down on the ground again.

Chappell was choking up at the sight, but waited for Darius to climb the porch stairs before she held out her arms for a hug. Darius smiled warmly and hugged his mother for a long moment, kissing her on the cheek as he let her go. Turning to his father, Darius held out his hand.

"Dad? How's it goin'?" he asked as they heartily shook hands.

"Fine, son. Look at ya'! Strong as an ox! What are they feedin' ya'?"

"The usual for a basketball playa'. It's not season yet, but we have to stay in shape even out of season, and I like it."

The whole family sat amiably on the porch together for the first time since Darius was eleven. The last time he had seen his family was the day after graduation when he had left to go to Richmond to find a job to help pay the tuition that his scholarship did not cover. Being the main attraction that day, Darius did most of the talking, and the more he talked about his college campus life, the more Lydia yearned to go to college when she graduated next year, but what kind of scholarship could she possibly get since she was not involved in sports? Her heart sank, and she grew somewhat quiet at the last of the conversation, finally excusing herself to go and fix supper for everyone.

Later that night, while sitting on the porch swing waiting for the bedroom to cool down enough to sleep in it, Darius and Lydia conversed about all that had transpired that summer between various family members, occasionally sadly chortling about the absurdity of the situation in which they had grown up, and being thankful that at last changes were happening that may bring some relief. It was after one of several conversational pauses that Lydia began to tell Darius what had happened to her at camp a couple of months ago, and how she now belonged to God, and that she knew Jesus as the one through whom all this was possible. She spoke of how much she loved Jesus and how much help He had been in some of her trials lately. She even told Darius about the Bible and its rescue from a fiery destruction in the cook stove. Darius listened quietly, looking down at the porch as the lazy swing glided back and forth, back and forth, the chain grinding rhythmically, creaking softly under its breath with each swing. Finally, he looked up at Lydia with a smile.

"You needed somethin' like that, didn't ya'? Man, I still kick myself when I think of the times that I ignored all you were goin' through just 'cause I wanted to be popular with those worthless snobs. I'm glad you've found somethin' to hold onto, Lydia."

"It's someone, Darius, not just some thing, and I didn't find Him, He found me, and He saved me from this world and everything in it."

"But you're still here, and though you and Mom are gettin' along, Dad still ignores ya'. How can ya' say that you've been saved from everything in this world when ya' still have to face the same world everyday?"

"I don't know how to explain it, I just know that all of what's goin' on 'round me no longer matters 'cause I know there is somethin' else out there for me, somethin' God has planned for me to do, and that gives me hope while I'm still here in this. Besides, once ya' know God, things here don't matter as much as things to come."

"What do ya' mean?"

"I mean that we're only here for a speck of time, and then we die, and afta' that we live eternally, so what comes afta' this life is what we focus on while we're in this life."

"Whoa! Ya' lost me back at 'speck of time'. Where're you getting' all this stuff?"

"From my Bible," she responded eagerly, "Ya' want me to go and git it?"

"Well, looks like we'll be out here for a while longer, so you might as well," he replied sniffing at her enthusiasm, "but don't expect me to git all involved in it like you are, ya' hear?"

Lydia jumped up and seized the front screen door handle, but then stopped and turned to face Darius with a look of hesitancy.

"I wasn't thinkin' just then, Darius. If Dad knows that I still have this Bible, he'll burn it for sure this time," She said and headed slowly back to the swing, but Darius stuck out his bulky shoe and wouldn't let her pass by.

"You let me worry 'bout that, now go git it," he grinned rascally.

Lydia laughed and slid stealthily through the screen door, closing it gently behind her in case her parents were already asleep. She was back in the swing within a few minutes with the precious book in her hand, and as she ardently read numerous passages to her brother, he kept the swing chains groaning by pushing lightly with his big feet. With each passage, Lydia's fervor grew until she had tears in her eyes as she spoke of her Lord and all His power and might. Darius listened without interrupting: sometimes with his head down, sometimes looking straight into Lydia's beautiful green eyes brimming with jubilant tears, always with that gathered brow which let Lydia know that he was really taking it all in, genuinely considering the Biblical enlightenment to which she was exposing him.

After about an hour of Bible reading and listening to Lydia's accounts of God's goodness to her, Darius abruptly reached out and pushed the Bible shut. Lydia, surprised by this atypical behavior, stared at him with her mouth poised to question his actions, but Darius took the Bible from Lydia and put it flat on the swing between them.

"I understand," he said, "but now I need to do somethin' 'bout it, don't I?" He got up from the swing, turned to face Lydia, and then dropped down on his knees, propping his elbows on the swing and cupping his face in his hands. Lydia watched at first, confused, until she heard him begin to pray, and then she understood and got on her knees beside him there on the porch.

"God, I've been so angry and so empty, and 'til now, didn't even know that it was you I was lonely for. Please forgive me for not comin' to ya' soona', and be in me like you're in Lydia. I need ya', too. Let me be yer child, God, and let me know Jesus." Darius wept as he prayed, but before long he was laughing with joy, throwing his arm around Lydia and hugging her to himself as together they praised God and laughed through their tears of salvation. They were now brother and sister in the Holy Spirit, and their joy was immeasurable.

Darius went back to Richmond the next morning, but before he went, he gave his father a bear hug and a kiss on the neck, making Earl rather uncomfortable, but pleased.

"I luv' ya', Dad, and I'll be prayin' for ya'."

"Yeah, son, now git on back 'fore it gits too dark to drive."

Lydia walked down the drive a long way waving at her brother until he pulled out onto the state road and disappeared behind the thick border of trees that defined their front property. Wow, she thought, God had heard her prayers for Darius, and now he was saved. She looked back toward the house at Chappell and Earl, still gazing up the road after Darius, and wondered if God would hear her prayers for her father when they were offered so reluctantly as there was still a part of her that wanted to see him suffer for all her had put her through. She shook her head to rid herself of the thought and headed back home. School would start soon, and she would be away from this place most of the time. Maybe then she would be able to honestly pray for her father, if she did not have to be around him so much.

School commenced on the third day of September, a Tuesday, and Lydia could not wait to get on the bus. Surely things would be wonderfully different in school this year having Jesus with her in that horrible place. Lydia boarded the school bus not realizing that the summer had transformed her into a taller, tanner, more appealing beauty than she had been in the spring. She never thought about those things until they were brought to her attention, and when someone emitted a low seductive whistle upon her entering the bus, she blushed and instinctively looked for the nearest empty seat in which to hide, but there weren't any in the front of the bus. She was being seized by her usual panic, when a voice seemed to whisper in her ear, "You are mine. Old things are passed away, and behold, all things have become new." Lydia stood still and listened to the words, calming her breath, allowing her heart to slow down its beats, looking each student in the eye as she panned the bus. Finally, spotting an empty seat, Lydia deftly sashayed to it and sat down next to a lovely blonde girl that she had never seen before.

"My name is Lydia. Do ya' mind if I sit here today?"

"No, not at all. I'm Nancy."

"Are ya' new this year?"

"Yes, we just moved here from South Boston. I'm not used to being in the country like this. We always lived in the city until now."

"You'll like it, don't worry," Lydia reassured the girl, and then smiled as she looked around at the familiar faces that stared back at her in disbelief. It was going to be a good year.

Lydia went to her locker in the East wing as soon as she got off the bus. She had thought about David a lot that summer, but unfortunately, not the way that she had thought she would, although the prospect of him still being interested in her after all this time were small. Nevertheless, David was waiting for her at her locker, and when he saw her, he was visibly taken back.

"Man, were you ever worth the wait!" he said, and before she could protest, he grabbed her and kissed her right on the mouth. "Wow, you look really great! He said again. "Your hair has gotten so much longer, and look at you! If you were pretty before, you're gorgeous now."

"Stop it! Ya' know I don't really have a mirra' at home, so I don't know what you're talkin' 'bout," she pulled his arms away from her and opened her locker.

"So? How was your summer?" he asked, not waiting for an answer. "Mine was terrific! I got to go hiking in the Appalachian mountains for a whole month with this group from my dad's office, a sort of father-son thing. So what did you do?"

"I got saved," Lydia blurted out while putting away her books.

"From what?"

She laughed, "You know, saved, like in now I belong to God."

David frowned.

"You aren't going to start preaching to me, are you, because I have some pretty fascinating plans for us for this year, and I wouldn't want anything to interfere with them, you know?" he winked at her.

"What sort of plans?"

"Can you meet me after school here? We'll talk about them then, okay?"

"I guess so. I'm on the second bus this year, so I have almost an hour to wait, so yeah, I'll be here. I need to talk to you, too."

The bell rang, and David stole another quick kiss from her before heading to class. Lydia suffered with guilt about the way she felt toward David now. Where had all her ardor for him gone? All she knew was at this point in her life, there was only one man with which she wanted to spend time, and that man was Jesus.

With each successive class, Lydia felt more confident in herself, and more comfortable in her own skin. She was not intimidated by the other students, for she saw them as people needing God in their lives, and as such, not responsible for the harm they had caused her. Though Lydia was still shy around strangers, and that included most of the students, she no longer felt bound by her panic attacks or embarrassment over her clothes, or her lack of riches. Lydia looked forward to this school year and hoped God would use her to pray for souls here as he had used her to pray for Darius.

At the last bell, Lydia headed toward her locker, but even after the other students had gotten their books and left for their buses, David had still not shown up. She was the only one in the hallway now, and stood leaning against the lockers with one foot propped up behind her. Finally, David came around the corner and walked briskly toward her, smiling as he got closer. He pushed her books out of her arms onto the floor, slid his arm around her waist, and drew her into him without even saying hello first, and the next thing Lydia knew, David was passionately kissing her while pressing her ever closer into his body. It was more seductive than anything Lydia had ever known, and she could not help but enjoy the sensation it gave her.

"That's my plan for this year," David breathed into her ear, "to make love to you, Lydia."

Lydia's mind was reeling with shock over this revelation, but a part of her glowed with pride that such a good looking young man would have these feelings for her. He kissed her again and began to run his hand down her body while holding her face in the grasp of his other hand so she could not resist his kiss. Lydia squirmed and tried to turn her face, but his grip was too strong. She grabbed his other arm with her free hand to stop him from groping at will over her body, but again, he overpowered her, and such was David's obsession with having her that he was oblivious to Lydia's efforts to stop him and to her salty tears running down into their mouths. Finally, in a frantic effort to get him off of her, Lydia worked her arms between them and pushed with all her might, kneeing him in the thigh to make him stop. He stepped backwards and glared at her.

"Bitch! What do you think you're doing?"

"Me? Who do ya' think you are that you can handle me that way? I thought we had somethin' special. I honestly believed you were differ'nt than all the other guys 'round here!" she cried.

"I'm no different than any other normal guy who's crazy about the girl he's with. I just want more, that's all. I want to be closer to you. I want to be as close as two people can get."

"That kind of closeness comes with marriage, David, and I don't think you have marriage in mind here," Lydia boiled over with anger and bawled up her fist to smash his face.

This was the worse insult she had ever received in her life. Those girls in the hallway had known all along. What a fool she had been for believing that a boy in David's social setting would really be in love with a girl from her side of the tracks. What a fool! Lydia wanted to fight and hide at the same time: fight this deceptive man standing in front of her, and hide from the shame of her foolishness. She turned to pick up her books, but as she was reaching down to stack them up, David grabbed her arm and jerked her up straight, slamming her against the lockers and pinning her there with his knee. With one arm across her chest and his other hand holding her wrist, he glowered at her in annoyance.

"Nobody walks away from me like that--nobody! Especially not someone like you. I nursed you along for a lot of embarrassing months, hung on all summer waiting for this moment, and now you think you're just going to walk away? You owe me! I made you acceptable around here, and now all I'm asking for is a little something in return," he tightened his grip on her wrist, "and I don't think that's too much to ask for."

Lydia was terrified, but no matter how hard she struggled, she could not free herself from his grasp. Something about this scenario ignited an old memory, and she instinctively knew how this would end if she could not break free, so Lydia began to call on God out loud.

"Father, help me!" she eked out amid her struggling.

David twisted his head to see if Lydia's father was behind him, and when he did, she had the opening she needed to fight. This time, she was not so merciful as to knee him in the thigh, but brought her knee hard against his groin, using the palm of her free hand to punch him in the face as she wrenched her other hand from his grip. He crumpled over in pain, and Lydia bolted towards the huge double steel doors at the end of the hallway. She would get her books tomorrow. Today she was free!

"Thank you, thank you, thank you," Lydia repeated as she ran out the door and headed to the bus stop, but before she could enjoy her victory, a colossal cloud of anguish rolled over her heart, and she could not breathe. Sweat began to pour from her body, and shaking, she retreated into the band room building to hide in the restroom. Lydia cried uncontrollably, her body racking with every sob. How would she ever face the students at this school again after David got through telling them what a freak she was? How could he have been so deceptive? Why wasn't she good enough for someone like him? This world was too hard a place for Lydia to endure, and once more she began to make plans to leave it. Forget God, forget Jesus, and forget trying to be a Christian, she thought. It was just impossible for someone like her to be a child of God. Impossible. It was for people like Mrs. Lorraine, and Mr. Landon, and even Darius who had what it took to be a good Christian, but she did not have the strength to do it. She would always be an embarrassment to God, and she did not think He would like that for very long.

Lydia decided to go back to her locker and get her books before going to the bus stop. David would be long gone, and what did it matter anyway? She dried her sad eyes, smoothed her hand-me-down clothes, and trod solemnly out the bathroom door, defeat written all over her face, resolve to die once again etched in her mind. At the bus stop, Lydia stood lost in thought when a hand suddenly thrust a piece of paper in front of her, and a senior girl said smiling, "Hi, I would like to invite you to our church."

Lydia looked back at the girl expressionless. It seemed to Lydia that every time she thought about dying, God would invite her to church.

Chapter Eleven

"**Y**ou know yer dad ain't goin' to take ya' to no church, Lydia, so there's no use askin'," Chappell explained when she read the brochure.

"But it's just up the road a bit," Lydia insisted.

"Well, then you may have to walk to it, but I sure wouldn't git yer dad all riled up by askin' him to take ya'."

Lydia folded the brochure and put it back inside her Bible. One way or another, she would get to a church on Sunday and listen to the preaching for herself and sing songs like she sang at camp earlier that summer. Now there was one more thing that Lydia had to discuss with her mother.

"I want a job after school," Lydia blurted out.

"What?"

"I want to get an after school job so I can buy a Bible that has all the pages in it," she explained.

Chappell furrowed her brow and tilted her head to one side.

"What makes ya' think yer Dad is goin' to agree to that? He's still upset 'bout me helpin' ya' with the chores as it is, not that I hafta' listen to him."

"I was hopin' you could talk to him for me," Lydia suggested.

Chappell tilted her head the other way, pursing her lips, then with a sigh said, "Oh, alright. I'll ask him, but don't hold yer breath."

Earl had no problem with Lydia working a public job as long as she could get herself to and from the job without him, and as long as she put half her paycheck into the family funds to make up for the money he had lost on her that summer. Lydia knew that she could ride the school bus down town to work, but how she would get back home at night, she did not yet know. Maybe there was a city bus she could ride out to the city limit and then walk home from there. It didn't matter. One way or another she would have a job. Lydia remembered a song from camp, "God can open a way where no way appears," and she made up her mind to pray for God to open a way for her to work to buy this Bible.

The next school day, Lydia was so preoccupied with the thoughts of finding a job that she was oblivious to the heckling crowd of David's friends who eventually grew tired of being ignored and found other more worthy pursuits. After school, she boarded an early bus and rode downtown where she got off in front of Woolworth's Department Store. Upon inquiring inside about a job, the lady behind the lunch counter informed her that they were not hiring, but that the drycleaners down the street was looking for a front girl. Lydia had no idea what a front girl was, but she was sure that she could learn to do anything they needed her to do, so she entered the cleaners and asked for an application. The young and handsome manager, whose name was Mike, took one look at her and gave her the job saying that she could fill out the application at home and bring it back with her tomorrow. Lydia joyfully took the application, thanked the manager profusely, and headed back up the street to Woolworth's where she planned to catch the late school bus to get home. As she was strolling up the street, Lydia noticed a store with Christian symbols on the front and decided to stop in and see if Bibles were sold there.

The store had such an array of Bibles, books, music, and other amazing Christian paraphernalia that Lydia just stood in the middle of the entrance as if in a trance until, finally, a saleswoman asked if she could help her, causing Lydia to blush and laugh nervously.

"I would just like to look at yer Bibles, please," she sputtered.

The salesclerk gave her a quick up and down visual assessment and then kindly said, "Our Bibles are of the highest print quality, and most are somewhat, well, expensive. May I show you our most economical line? It is the basic King James Version in the old text format, but it is very reasonably priced."

"I would like a Bible like the one Mrs. Lorraine has with extra notes in the middle, and other study verses, ya' know? One that can help me really understand the Bible," Lydia explained humbly.

"Well, those are the ones that are going to cost a lot more, dear, but if you would like to see them, just come this way, please."

The two ladies crossed to an isle with what seemed like a hundred Bibles on display in every conceivable size, shape, and color. At the sight of them, Lydia's throat tightened, and tears welled up in her eyes as the salesclerk described the Bibles to her, allowing her to handle each copy as she praised its contents. Lydia's heart yearned to open them all and sit down right there and read them, but when she was handed a red leather Scoffield Bible, she knew that was the one she wanted.

"How much is this Bible?" she asked.

"That is a very nice Bible, and because it is, it costs $27.00, plus sales tax," she told her, then seeing the shocked look on Lydia's face, she added, "It's the leather cover."

Lydia swallowed hard. In those days, that was a lot of money for a book of any kind, and she would have to work a long time to afford it. Lydia caressed the Bible to her chest and silently prayed for God to help her to be able to buy it.

"You know, we have a lay-a-way plan," the saleslady offered sweetly.

"What is that?"

"Well, you put a few dollars down on the Bible, and then we keep it here until you have the whole thing paid for, and that way, you know for sure that the Bible will be here for you."

Lydia explained to the lady about her job with the dry cleaners down the street, and together they came up with a plan for Lydia to put several dollars down out of her first pay check and then to pay a little every week until the Bible was paid off. In the meantime, the compassionate lady agreed to hold the Bible behind the counter for Lydia until she got her first paycheck. Lydia hugged the salesclerk robustly, thanking her for everything, and then strode gleefully out of the door to catch the bus.

Holding an afterschool job proved to be more of a challenge than Lydia had expected. Fortunately, one of the other women who worked at the cleaners lived out in the county near her and so offered her a ride home at night for which Lydia paid her gas money each week. Upon arriving at home, she did the chores that were left for her around the house, and then in the remaining time before lights out, Lydia worked on her homework leaving her no time to read her Bible before going to sleep. The mornings seemed to come extra early, and getting out of bed became harder and harder each day, but Lydia soon got used to the grueling schedule, and as she got faster at her front job at the cleaners, Mike allowed her to work on homework between customers, as long as she made no mistakes writing up the clothes. This left Lydia some time at night for reading and studying her Bible.

At $3.00 per hour, Lydia's weekly pay was already meager, and after tax deductions, and after setting aside ten per cent to give to church for tithe--which she had learned at church was her duty--

and after giving away several dollars for gas money, and giving half of the original amount to her father, Lydia was left with only a few dollars each week to hand to the wonderful salesclerk to pay for the Bible. Thus, it was about four and a half months before Lydia was able to actually walk out of the store with her prized possession, and the salesclerk was so proud of her that she gave Lydia a thin, fancy, brass book marker for free to use with her new Bible. It was one of the most wonderful days in Lydia's austere life!

The longer Lydia attended the Green Grove Christian Church, the more the youth director, Mr. Mavlin, hounded her about attending a Christian college upon graduating from high school, and when he planned a trip to visit a small Bible college in Winston-Salem (a town just over the state line), he visited Lydia's house to convince her parents to allow her to go with the youth group on this trip. Even Earl could not resist this fervent young director, nor could he come up with a good excuse why Lydia could not go, except for the impossibility of paying for any college, but the director locked the deal by uttering the irrefutable truth that whatever God wanted Lydia to do, He would supply the way to do it. Who could argue with that?

Lydia was elated, and when Saturday morning arrived, she was up before the sun eating a hearty breakfast when Chappell shuffled into the kitchen sleepy-eyed, stopping to gaze at the plate of bacon and basket full of biscuits that were already cooked for her and Earl. Lydia put her plate into the warm dishwater in the pan on the large wood cook stove, hugged Chappell goodbye, and grabbed her new Bible before heading out the back door to walk the thirty minutes up the road to the church. The bus was already loaded when she got there.

"Man, I thought you had changed your mind, girl!" shouted the youth director as he waved to her from the bus steps. Lydia hopped onto the bus and sat in a seat by herself as she did not feel that she knew any of the other youth well enough to impose on them. However, several of the girls from further back in the bus came up and sat around her and one in the seat with her to talk, and before long, she felt very much a part of that little group of girls, though she was ever conscious of how nice their clothes and shoes were next to hers. Though these girls did not seem to notice, Lydia's experience with David still stung her heart, and she found herself holding back with these new acquaintances just in case their intentions were not as honorable as they seemed. It had always been hard for her to look people in the eyes, or carry on a conversation without stuttering, so Lydia mostly listened and smiled appropriately at their chatter, being careful not to think too much of this friendliness; they were just doing their Christian duty.

To say the college was small was an understatement. Just shy of three hundred students, the little school took up one city block with a church across the street from which it had originated. The campus was small but quaint, and Lydia took an immediate liking to it. They spent the day roaming through the dorms and classrooms, meeting the students and some of the teachers, and playing ping-pong in the student lounge where Lydia found out she was somewhat athletic after all, but when people started to gather to watch her play, she succumbed to her usual panic attack and excused herself to go to the lady's room. She stayed there a long while until she had calmed down, but Lydia was too embarrassed to go back out until one of the girls from the youth group knocked on the door to check on her.

"Lydia, you okay? We're going to supper now, come on!"

Lydia opened the door, smiling at the girl, and left with her to join the others for a last meal at the college before heading back home. It had been a good day, and now she could see why Mr. Mavlin wanted to see the members of his youth group go to a Christian college, even though only three programs were offered at the time. Lydia had fallen in love with the place, but at the informational meeting the cost of the school, along with all the other incidental costs, had been given to them as part of a prospective student package, and Lydia could do the math. With the money she was making now, it would take her about eight years to save up enough money for one year of college, so she sat quietly to herself on the bus, occasionally brushing a tear from her cheek, listening to the other students excitedly making plans to attend college when they graduated.

Mike, the manager at the cleaners, had become quite fond of Lydia, and frequently praised her work ethic, saying that he never had to go behind her and correct anything that she did. As her high school graduation grew nearer, he began to hint around about making her assistant manager on a full time basis.

"I tell you, Lydia, I can use someone like you around here on a daily basis to oversee the front and pressers. What do you say? The pay is great, and you even get medical benefits. How can you turn that down?"

"I want to go to college like my brotha'."

"Yeah, but he got his way paid with basketball. How you gonna' get your money, huh? I'll tell you how--working here for a couple of years and putting the money into a savings account, that's how. It's a good deal I'm offering you, girl, and I honestly think you'd do a bang up job as assistant manager," Mike said convincingly.

"You're really sweet to offa' me this, Mike, and if August comes 'round, and I don't have a way to college by then, I'll sure take ya' up on it. Deal?"

"You bet it's a deal, and I'm holding you to it," he laughed and sauntered back into the steamy depths of the cleaners, gathering an armful of clothes out of the bin up front as he passed by, whistling an old hymn from his church hymnal as he went.

Lydia had money to rent her own cap and gown, and to buy her tassel. Both her parents and Darius were present to watch her receive her diploma, but there were no pictures taken as there had been none taken at Darius's graduation. They were not a family into saving memories from the past. Nevertheless, between Darius and Lydia, the whole family was able to go to the ice cream shop down town and each buy a bowl of chocolate mocha. Mike had not been able to come to the graduation, but had given Lydia a gift of $50.00 towards her college fund, and the wonderful salesclerk, who had become friends with Lydia during the school year, also gave her a gift of $30.00 for college. Her church had given her a devotional book and a gift of $10.00, so Lydia's college fund was growing, and so were her hopes. Darius gave her a guitar and a book to learn how to play it. She was totally surprised, but utterly pleased. Now she could sing all her beloved church songs at home all week!

"I knew you'd like it," Darius announced proudly, " 'cause you've always loved music, and I've heard ya' sing. Who knows, maybe you'll be famous one day," he laughed.

"Well, Lydia, now that you've graduated, you can work full time and really help out the family," Earl stated.

Chappell sighed and looked down as if to avoid facing an inevitable clash, and Darius cleared his throat. The fact that Lydia wanted to go to college was known by everyone in the family, even Earl, but for some reason, he had chosen to go down this route with her tonight, knowing it would lead to an argument and spoil an otherwise peaceful evening.

Lydia looked at him, opened her mouth, but then decided against speaking, and resumed eating her ice cream. Darius smiled at her and pinched her under the table, giving her the thumbs up sign where his father would not see it. Chappell also smiled at Lydia, thanking her with her eyes for not taking the bait. Earl looked back and forth between Darius, Lydia, and Chappell, knowing he had been outdone, but not really wanting to pursue it any further that night. He would wait until Lydia came to him for help with tuition, then he would get the last laugh, then he would have the last word.

At church the Sunday after graduation, Mr. Mavlin met Lydia in the vestibule as she entered, and ushered her to the side, whispering excitedly in her ear as they walked about money for school.

"I'm sorry, Mr. Mavlin, but I can't understand a word you're sayin'," she whispered. "Tell me again?"

"Well, I don't want to speak too loudly because it is kind of a secret thing we're doing, and certain people in the church might take it the wrong way, but there is a group of members who have been following your growth in the Lord, Lydia, and have watched your faithfulness to the church, and who know of your desire to go to Bible college, and well, they have taken up a collection for you for just that purpose--three thousand, two hundred twenty-seven dollars--enough to pay for your first year at school!"

"What...?" Lydia was not sure she had heard correctly.

"Here, see for yourself!" he said, and showed her the check for the huge amount.

Her eyes grew large, and she couldn't breathe. There was a ringing in her ears, and then everything went black as Lydia passed out right there in the vestibule. Later, on the bench in front of the coat closet, and away from prying eyes, Mr. Mavlin and his wife again handed the check to Lydia, who broke down and wept, hugging them both until they could not breathe.

"I can't believe it! I just can't believe it! God is so good. How can I eva' thank everyone who did this for me?"

"Well, they choose to remain anonymous, Lydia, so you'll have to just send a card to them through us, and we'll make sure they understand how grateful you are, and Lydia, if you do well in college, there may just be more donations later," the youth director and his wife beamed at her with pride, and then offered to give her a ride home after church to help her explain the money to her parents.

The look on Earl's face when he saw the check was priceless to Lydia. He was truly shaken by the generosity of the church toward his daughter, though he could not understand for sure why they were being so generous to her, and he kept questioning Mr. Mavlin. It also took the wind out of his sails because now he had nothing to hold over Lydia's head come fall.

"This only pays fer one year, don't it? How's she s'posed to pay fer the other three?" he inquired, hoping there would not be an answer.

"I am sure Lydia can get one or perhaps two campus jobs which will pay enough to cover most of the tuition; otherwise, she'll have to pray for more donations, won't she?" quipped Mr. Mavlin chuckling. Earl did not respond to his humor.

"Well, I don't like my daughter begging for money, or taking handouts," he complained.

"I assure you, Mr. Marshall, this is not a …"

"I call it a hand out, and I don't like it," Earl snapped leaving the director and his wife feeling awkward and wondering if they should leave.

"Well, I do," chimed in Chappell, "and the more she can git, the betta'. It's a gift 'cause they see promise in our little girl, and that's more than I can say fer you, Earl," Chappell turned to Lydia. "Ya' take whateva' anyone gives ya', and ya' see it as a gift from God, ya' hear?" She then turned to the youth director, putting her hand on his arm. "Thank ya' fer all ya' do fer Lydia, 'specially this. It's a dream come true fer her, and no one deserves a dream as much as Lydia."

It was settled. Lydia was going to college in the fall. She would have to work while attending classes in order to save money for the next year, but Lydia had grown up working and saw no problem with it. Her boss, Mike, was visibly disappointed, but somewhat fascinated that all of a sudden, Lydia's money was there, like a miracle or something.

"It was a miracle! God laid it on the hearts of all those people to do this. Neat, huh?" Lydia glowed in the absolutely marvelous way that God had provided her money, sure proof that He wanted her to go to college.

Darius came home that fall in order to drive Lydia to her college and help her get settled. She had only her gunnysack of clothes, towels, sheets, blankets, and a pillow, and upon seeing all the household items her three roommates had, Lydia's heart sank. What would they think of their dirt poor roommate? This was a part of college to which she had given no thought, and now here she was, being thrust into the situation cold turkey, and she could already feel her chest getting tighter. Darius put his hand on her shoulder and pushed her into the door to meet the roomies. She waved feebly and smiled.

"Hi! You must be Lydia. I'm Cindy, that's Louise, and here is Daniele," she laughed dragging Daniele off the bottom bunk on which she was resting. They all came over and shook hands with her, then all their attention turned to Darius.

"Your brother?" Cindy asked holding out her hand. "Pleased to meet you," she cooed, smiling at him.

"Pleasure's all mine, Miss Cindy," Darius responded suavely, shaking her hand while never losing eye contact. "Well, Lydia, looks like you're in good hands here, so I'll be getting back to my own school. Ladies?"

Lydia walked him out to his car.

"I don't know how to thank ya', Darius, but I'm not sure I'm goin' to be able to stay here. I feel so...wrong fer this place, ya' know, like I ain't good enough to associate with these people," she explained and tears began to well up in her eyes.

Darius took her beautiful face in his strong hands and, speaking firmly to her, said, "Lydia, this school, these people, aren't worthy of you, and don't ya' eva' forget that. You stay, and neva' give up, and keep yer eyes on Jesus, not the people 'round ya', and you'll do just fine. I'm very proud of ya'."

They hugged each other for a long time, and then Darius got into his car and drove away, leaving Lydia once again in a strange new world to fend for herself, only this time, in spirit, he was with her.

Chapter Twelve

The small college offered only three degrees, one of which was a Bachelor of Religious Education which was the program of study Lydia chose to embark upon, choosing a music minor to complete her credits. As a music student, she was required to take voice lessons and music theory, and to participate in the traveling choir in which she sang soprano. Her other classes revolved around basic academics, Christian teaching methodology, and theology studies, her personal favorites. When she was not in class, Lydia was working in the cafeteria, in the snack shop, or in the bookstore.

Once a week, all voice students had to sing in front of each other in a performance class designed to allow one's peers to critique one's vocal progress, but Lydia, who did so well singing alone in the practice room with her guitar, or in the shower, found it impossible to relax and sing in front of her instructor in private lessons, or in front of the class on Mondays. She would visibly shake and not be able to take in enough air to support the notes in the difficult music her instructor, Mr. Sutton, had given her, and so would be mortified at the end of each piece of music sung in front of the class when all would tell her what she already knew: let go, breathe, and enjoy singing. It was her biggest struggle all year, yet in her other classes, Lydia did well and built for herself quite a reputation for her Bible knowledge and her ability to pray with so much ease.

Sometimes at night, when all was quiet and her roommates were asleep, Lydia would sneak out of the dorm and trek down to the nearby park just to sit undetected in the shadows of the trees and listen to the night noises she missed so much from her country home. It was forbidden by the rules, but her occasional need to escape so outweighed her fear of the forbidden that she indulged herself in this one infringement, hoping God would understand and not let her get caught.

It was on one such night, sitting alone in the deep shadow of an oak that Lydia witnessed a scene that made her blood curdle. Two men entered the park from across the little bridge opposite the tree under which Lydia was concealed, and they were dragging along a reluctant teenage boy, cursing to his face as they went. About half way between the bridge and Lydia's hiding place, they stopped and confronted the boy.

"You have one more chance to give it up, now where is it?"

"I don't know," the boy pleaded, but one of the men kneed him hard in the stomach.

"I'm gettin' tired of this. Let's just finish him here," the other man suggested.

"No, wait, honest, I don't know," the boy wailed falling on his knees.

"Too bad," said the first guy and raised a long black stick to strike the boy on the head.

"No!" screamed Lydia without thinking. Then realizing what she had done, she froze in the shadow of the tree, slowly lowering her head and allowing her long hair to cover most of her face so whatever traces of light streaming down from the moon would not reflect on her sweaty skin and give her away.

"What the…" both men whirled around and searched the darkness walking in her direction. She knew from years of playing hide and seek at night with her brother that if she sat perfectly still with her legs stretched out in the shadow, the men would not be able to see her. Sure enough, they walked right past her several times in vain, beating at the large bushes to each side of her, but never knowing she was there.

"Let's get outta' here…where did he go, the little punk?" In all the excitement, the teenage boy had slipped away to safety, at least for now. The men walked briskly away, looking back now and then in Lydia's direction to see if there really was someone there, but finally disappearing over the bridge and up the street out of sight. Lydia sat still a long time just in case they were watching, then made her way back to the dorm using the shadow of trees in which to conceal her travel until she was safely back on campus and in her bed. She prayed for the teenage boy's safety, and then reluctantly prayed for the salvation of the two men, and for God to forgive her for being so foolish. It was the last time that Lydia left the dorm after hours.

No matter how much she loved the school, as time passed Lydia felt more and more out of place and found herself withdrawing from activities and people around her, spending too much time in her room or at work. School assignments usurped so much of her time with jobs filling in the empty gaps that Lydia hardly had time for her own Bible study and prayer, and as a result, did not feel the presence of God with her as she was accustomed. Her roommates began doing most things without her, and the other students, unacquainted with the symptoms of depression, soon backed away to accommodate her sad, dark disposition.

Occasionally, Lydia would have a Sunday afternoon off, and she would take her guitar to a practice room in the music building and sing wonderful, meaningful, old hymns memorized from her church hymnal, or songs that she had written herself. The walls of the music room were somewhat sound proof, but Lydia's strong, rich voice could penetrate the barrier and still be heard by people on the sidewalk, or in other practice rooms, and often, unbeknown to Lydia, she would have an audience during her praise and worship sessions, including Mr. Sutton and his wife who would sit on the steps of the music building and listen in awe, wondering why she could not do that in front of people, and praying for a way to help that confidence surface in her.

"Too bad she can't sing with her guitar in class," Mrs. Sutton casually remarked to her husband during one of Lydia's private Sunday afternoon concerts.

"What? What did you say, honey?" her husband sat upright and stared at his wife.

"I said, it's too bad she can't use her guitar in class. She seems to be so at ease with it, and to be able to really express her heart when she sings this way."

"There are policies about using guitars in the chapel and other places on campus, you know, because of its use in rock music."

"I'm not hearing rock music, dear; I'm hearing worship music, and some of the sweetest music I've ever heard. Why, I don't even recognize some of her songs. Do you think she wrote them herself?"

Mr. Sutton scratched his head, "I've never heard them, either. What if she did write them? What if the only way she can sing them is with the guitar because there is no sheet music for them anywhere? Honey, you're a genius! I'm going to get my recorder out of the car. I'll be right back!" he said, and scurried away like a man on a mission.

Soon, Lydia's songs were wafting through the air of the college President's office where the members of the school board and the presiding officers were trying to decide whether the use of a guitar in church was ungodly, or if the guitar could be used as an instrument of worship given some concessions. After listening to several songs, the board decided that the message of the songs far outweighed the prejudice toward using stringed instruments in worship, and amended the college policies to allow selective use of guitars on the school campus and in the chapel services, but it would be up to the Dean of Music to judiciously decide the proper use of these instruments. Mr. Sutton was elated!

Suddenly, Lydia was plunged into an arena the likes of which she would never have sought. Mr. Sutton asked her to sing her songs for her classmates in Monday's class using her guitar, and though it was easier for Lydia to sing this way, she had mixed feelings about sharing with strangers words that had come straight from the desperation of her soul and which had been intended for God's ears only, yet she did, and the results overwhelmed her. Upon finishing her song, Lydia's peers left their seats and gathered around her, hugging her and thanking her for the words of the song which so aptly expressed their own unspoken desperations and the hope they too could find in surrender and honesty before Jesus.

Until then, Lydia had mistakenly believed that everyone around her was always happy and had no problems to deal with, at least none that were apparent. Now she realized that much pain could be masked with a smile, rather than being acknowledged before God where one could find healing, but Lydia also realized the value of smiling before people while unmasking pain before God. Why let negative feelings and despair be evident to others?

Why not leave the burden of personal despair with God, and thus be approachable to help shoulder the burden of others? It was like a light went on in the core of Lydia's heart, and from that point on, she smiled and focused on the well-being of the students around her instead of being lost in her own self-centered emotions which she could cast regularly on God as the apostle Peter had admonished Christians to do. Lydia decided to rise and fellowship with God in prayer early in the mornings before work, no matter how sleepy she was. It became a lifetime habit.

One day at lunch, in the week before the spring break, while Lydia was serving plates in the cafeteria, Mr. Sutton came in and whispered something to the cafeteria manager who promptly took Lydia's place on the line, pointing toward Mr. Sutton. She untied her apron as she walked to where Mr. Sutton was waiting for her, and together they sat at a table in the middle of the loud, bustling cafeteria.

"I have such exciting news for you, Lydia!" he began breathlessly. "A group of five Christian businessmen would like to record your songs!"

"What do ya' mean?" Lydia was baffled.

"I mean, they would like for you to sing your songs on a record, and Lydia, they are willing to pay for everything: the music arrangements, the recording studio, back up singers, the travel…"

"Travel?" she was still confused.

"Yes, Lydia, you would be able to go around the country and sing in many, many churches, auditoriums, and gatherings of all kinds. Why, it's such an amazing opportunity! I can't believe it, can you?"

"No, sir, I can't... believe it, that is. I don't know what to say. When do they want all this?"

"Whenever you're ready, and we figured you'd want to finish the school year before really jumping into it. Lydia, this kind of opportunity doesn't come along but once in a lifetime," Mr. Sutton was very convincing.

"I have to talk with my parents, ya' know, but we leave this weekend for choir tour, so I can't even talk to 'em 'til I get back. Can I pray 'bout all this? I really need to pray," Lydia stated flatly.

"What's to pray about? God gave you the voice. God gave you the songs. God is now giving you an opportunity to use the voice and the songs for His glory, right? Besides, Lydia, you would have more than enough money to pay for college when you came back from tour."

"Tour?"

"I'm so happy for you, girl, but you go and pray about it now, and I just know that God will tell you what the rest of us already know. Say, why don't I write a letter to your parents about this so they can be thinking about it while you're on tour? Good plan!" he decided, patting her on the back, and walked away chuckling with genuine happiness for his student.

Lydia's head was spinning as she returned to her place in the serving line, and she was clearly distracted, putting the wrong food on the wrong plates and having to apologize for spilling drinks. Finally, her manager pulled her aside and excused her from the rest of the day's schedule, calling her back to him when she attempted to walk out still wearing her apron.

Lydia trudged straight to her room, plopped face down onto her thin mattress, and prayed until she fell asleep on her bunk. The room was dark and quiet when Lydia awoke hours later, and only the moonbeams spilling through the cracks in the blinds offered any light to the blurry eyed girl. She sat up at the head of the bed, bawling her legs up under her, and pulled the tiny string that opened the slats of the white metal blinds to reveal a cheerful full moon.

"It's like ya' put on a face so I can see ya'," Lydia smiled as she spoke to God. Then she thought about Jesus, the actual face of God, and remembered how she had seen that lovely face, and how He had sealed her adoption into His holy family. "I love ya', Jesus, and I don't mean to always be such a burden to ya', but it just seems like every time I turn around, somethin' else comes up. You heard Mr. Sutton… is this really what ya' want for me? Is this really goin' to be my purpose in life? Then why don't I feel some, I don't know, some joy over it?" Lydia sigh and waited in the stillness, gazing at the moon, listening for some guidance, but there was none, at least none that she could discern. She stretched out her aching legs and prepared to freshen up and get some supper before punching in at work, but before she arose, she took one more look at the moon.

"I'll just know, won't I, Lord?" she asked smiling, and then went about the business of getting dressed for her job at the snack shop, humming one of the songs He had given her for just such an occasion.

Chapter Thirteen

The choir returned home from tour on Friday of the week of spring break, and Lydia hitched a ride home with a couple of students headed to Arlington to visit their families before classes began again on Monday. She got them to drop her off at the end of her long dirt drive, and throwing her gunny sack over her shoulder, Lydia headed down the trail toward the house, hoping that her parents had gotten Mr. Sutton's letter so she would not have so much explaining to do. Sure enough, Chappell saw her coming and came out to the porch to greet her with hugs and congratulations. Earl, however, stayed inside leaning against the wall in a ladder-backed, straw-bottomed oak chair, waiting for her to come inside, and then he got up and left the front room to sit at the table in the kitchen, the place where family matters were usually settled. The ladies followed him, sitting across from him at the table after Chappell got Lydia a cup of coffee from the stove.

Looking around the room, Lydia realized that she did not miss this place at all. The oppression was palpable and though she had only been there a few minutes, her chest felt heavy with grief and regrets, and she fought the urge to go outside and draw a deep, refreshing breath. Chappell chattered on about school, asking Lydia how she liked everything, if her grades were good, if she was happy there. To all the questions, Lydia smiled feebly and shook her head yes. Her father watched this interaction with detachment until he could not take the dribble anymore.

"So Lydia, we've neva' heard ya' sing--eva', much less play yer guitar, and now all of a sudden, you're goin' to be a star. How's that happen?" Earl asked sarcastically.

Lydia impulsively looked down, "I don't know. Some people heard my songs and..." she began, but her father was not really interested in an answer.

"What songs? You a song writa', too, now? Boy, will wondas' neva' cease?" he laughed wickedly and slammed his palm down on the table top. "Oh yeah, I 'member the letta' talkin' 'bout yer songs, the letta' from some strange man tellin' me 'bout my daughta's activities. Why couldn't you have told us, huh? Why did we hafta' hear 'bout this from a stranger?" Earl's voice was rising.

"Earl, quit makin' such a fuss ova' nothin'," scolded Chappell.

"No, Mom, I can tell 'im," Lydia raised her head and looked directly at her father, a bit of enmity giving her the courage to do so. "It's 'cause I spend ev'ry minute of ev'ry day, includin' weekends either in class, in the libr'ry doin' homework, or at one of my three jobs. I don't have time to write nobody, or I'd sure write more to Darius. Mr. Sutton was doin' me a big faver, and I appreciated it."

"There! You satisfied? Lydia, neva' mind him; tell me 'bout yer singin' and 'bout this recordin' contract we read about," Chappell gushed.

"Mom, I don't know if I'm goin' to do it yet…"

"What do ya' mean, ya' don't know?" bellowed Earl, standing up at the table. "Ya' have a chance to make some real money, a chance to really help us out, and you're thinkin' of turnin' it down?" he asked incredulously.

"I don't have a peace about it yet, and I ain't doin' nothin' I don't have a peace about. There's some things more important than money…" Lydia tried to explain, but her father would have none of it.

"To hell with yer peace! I don't believe this!" he shouted shoving his chair back into the wall and stomping out of the kitchen. Lydia winced as the back door slammed into the side of the house before crashing shut again. She wished that she had never come home.

"Pay 'im no mind, Lydia. His mind is always on money and how to get more of it. It would be a shame, though, to have a chance to do somethin' so glamorous and not take advantage of it, don't ya' think?"

"Mom, don't."

"I'm just sayin' ya' ought to really pray earnestly 'bout it 'fore makin' up yer mind, that's all," Chappell said and patted her daughter on the back before getting up to clear the table. Lydia sighed and went to her room to lie down.

The rest of the weekend went by slowly with Lydia and her father avoiding each other like the plague. On Saturday morning, Lydia spent some time helping her mother with chores around the house, but that afternoon she escaped for a long period of time into the woods where she and her dog used to roam around exploring when she was little. Her dog had vanished when she was nine, just a little while after her mother's abrupt and mysterious departure, and she had often wondered what became of him. Now treading softly along the old familiar trails, observing the scattered streams of sunlight struggling to force their way down to the dark forest floor, Duke's unexplained disappearance haunted her intensely as did the memories of the day her mother left. What had happened, and how was Lydia involved?

Lydia trudged further down the overgrown trails into the heart of the lush woods until she came across a furrowed field full of weeds whose neat rows had been long untended. Strange, she thought, that a planting field would be stuck out here in the middle of nowhere. The emotional weight of trying to solve her past trauma wearied Lydia, and she sat on a moss covered stump at the edge of the forlorn field with her eyes closed to ponder the events of that rueful day, turning over as many small details in her mind as she could muster. She had slept out in the porch bedroom instead of her room. Why? She was still in her school clothes that morning, but her dress was dirty and torn. There were cuts and scratches on her body, and bruises around her throat. Why? Why? Lydia's mind reeled from its attempt to recall more than the obvious. That morning her father and brother were angry with her, yet no one told her why, and she hurt everywhere in her body. "Oh God, help me remember!" she implored, falling to her knees on the mulch laden ground with her face in her hands, "Help me understand! Please, set me free from this exhausting guilt, I beg ya', in the name of Jesus. Please!" she cried out loud, "I just can't bear it anymore."

Mr. Woodall. The name intruded into Lydia's memory.

Lydia's eyes flew open and she was stricken with terror. She rose slowly and, poised to run, she scrutinized the woods around her to see her assailant, but there was no one visible. Her eyes filled with tears as she began to stumble back down the path, blinded by fear, looking over her shoulder as she went, desperately seeking the fastest way out of the woods. Her face and arms were scratched by briars from wild roses and low hanging branches of the Hawthorne trees, and her blouse snagged and tore on a stub of a branch sticking out the side of a small maple tree, yet Lydia pressed onward, afraid to stop, until she reached the edge of the yard. Instinctively, she looked for her mother through the kitchen window, but her mother was not standing there at the work table. In that moment, a nine year old Lydia staggered to the house and crawled under the back porch stairs where she curled up into a tiny ball and slipped into the safe blackness of her unconscious mind.

"Lydia! Lydia!" her mother was sobbing as she plodded down the dirt drive still looking for her little girl with her frightened son by her side clenching her hand. The two of them had searched everywhere around the house, but it was getting dark, and her eyes were swollen from crying so that she could not see well anymore. Her husband and the sheriff's men were searching the woods and nearby farms. In a faraway field, they had found Lydia's sash caught on a thorn next to a short deep ditch filled with loose dirt clogs, and next to it was a shovel with dried blood on the curved side of the spade.

"I know who's shovel this is! Bastard!" Earl screamed, desperately searching the surrounding area. "Lydia! Oh, God, where is she?" he crumpled on the ground wailing for his daughter.

"Maybe you should go on home, now, Earl. You may not want to be here when we find her..." the sheriff knew he had said too much.

"Oh, God," he sobbed, "she just can't be dead."

"You just go on home now, ya' hear?" the sheriff gently patted him on the back and then helped him to his feet. They were turning to leave when a low groan emanating from the trees at the edge of the field made them freeze in their tracks.

Whirling around, Earl cried out, "Lydia?!" and raced back toward the edge of the woods at the side of the mysterious ditch.

"Lydia!" he cried out again, climbing through the brush, but the closer he came to the groaning, the more he smelled sour liquor, and his rage surged.

"Bastard! I'm gonna' kill ya!" Earl shrieked and plowed his way through the underbrush to pulverize to death the drunken man he held responsible for Lydia's disappearance, and the sheriff could not get there in time to prevent Earl from causing quite a bit of damage to Mr. Woodall's face before being held back by several strong, but reluctant deputies.

"What'd ya' have to go and do that for, you idiot? He was comin' to! He coulda' taken us to Lydia, but now we'll have to waste valuable time waitin' for him to come to again," the sheriff took off his hat and wiped his brow. "I can't say that I blame ya' none, Earl, but I'm goin' to hafta' take ya' in on charges of battery…"

"Me?!"

"Yes, you! This man is just laying here drunk and there's no evidence that he's had anything to do with Lydia's disappearance."

"That's his shovel!" Earl tried to point, but the deputies still had a tight hold on him, "and that may be Lydia's blood on it, and the sash…"

"All circumstantial. Now I'm gonna' hold ya' ova' night for yer own good, Earl. We'll keep looking for her, but you're goin' to jail. Take him, Joe."

"I can't believe this! I can't believe this!" Earl was crying and passive as the deputy placed his hand on Earl's head and helped him into the patrol car.

The darkness prevented Chappell and Darius from searching anymore, and a sobbing, weak woman and distraught little boy trudged reluctantly back toward the house. Under the steps, Lydia's unconscious mind heard distant crying, and she focused on the noise to discern who it was until, unexpectantly, her eyes opened, and she realized the crying was real, and that it was her mother and Darius sadly weeping, but where were they? Lydia slowly moved her aching head and looked around in the darkness. By the light of the moon, she could make out the slabs of the wooden steps above her, but her mind was so foggy, and her head hurt so badly, that Lydia could distinguish no more. Her mother and brother were about twenty yards from the back door, when Lydia crawled out from under the steps and began staggering toward them, holding her head with one hand, and reaching out like a zombie with the other.

Chappell and Darius stopped dead in their tracks, gaping in shock at the little specter coming at them in the darkness. Chappell could not breathe, and Darius cowered wide-eyed next to her holding onto her skirt, but until Lydia stepped out into the moonlight, neither one really believed that it was her, alive.

"Lydia!" Chappell cried out and, together with her son, ran at Lydia and scooped her up in her trembling arms, hugging her so closely that Lydia cried out with pain. Chappell was laughing hysterically and kissing Lydia over and over on her face when the sheriff drove up in the yard.

"My God!" he exclaimed.

"Yes!" Chappell laughed at him. "She's alive and home!"

The sheriff took Lydia in his arms and carried her into the kitchen and sat her on the kitchen table. A kerosene lantern was lit and brought to the end of the table so Chappell and the sheriff could see if the girl was injured, but as the light fell on her daughter, Chappell gasped, covering her mouth with her hands. Darius, too, let out an involuntary yell. The sheriff straightened his shoulders and prepared to be in charge of the situation.

"Now don't go jumpin' to any conclusions, Chappell. Let me go fetch 'doc for ya'. He'll be able to tell for sure," The sheriff said, and then put his hand on the stricken mother's shoulder. "Ya' know ya' can't wash her up or nothin' yet, right?"

Chappell shook her head up and down in acknowledgement, but kept staring at Lydia with a blank expression.

"Don't touch a thing, ya' hear me?"

Chappell once again shook her head in acknowledgement.

"Boy, ya' make sure yer mom don't do nothin' 'til I git back," he ordered the child, then headed quickly out the door.

"Yessir!" Darius promised and then reached for his mother's hand, but she would not have it. She curled both hands up into fists and went and sat down in a straw bottomed chair to wait for the sheriff's return, still staring strangely at her poor daughter.

Lydia tried to keep her eyes open as she continued to sit on the hard table, but exhaustion overcame her, and she curled up in a ball and slept. Darius, who had not left his spot, was torn between getting a blanket for his sister, and keeping watch over his mother. He soon decided that his mother was not going to do anything, so he trotted into the bedroom shared by him and his sister, and grabbed a blanket and a pillow off her bed. Lydia scrunched up comfortably when he put the pillow under her head and the blanket over her tiny shivering body. Now, he thought, everything's going to be alright, and he allowed himself to sit down next to the large cook stove where he could see both his mother and Lydia at the same time.

It was only about a half an hour before the sheriff returned. He was followed by another sheriff's vehicle, but the occupants of the second vehicle remained in the car parked under the mighty oaks in the side yard. The sheriff and Doc hurried into the back door and Doc slammed his black bag on the kitchen table startling Lydia from her sleep. His wife entered next with a solemn expression on her face, taking off her sweater and placing it over the back of a chair.

"Mrs. Marshall, Darius, you need to step outside," Doc demanded.

Darius and his mother looked at each other.

"Now, please!" Doc bellowed.

Darius rushed over to his mother and took her by the arm, escorting her toward the back door. Lydia whimpered and held out her arms for her mother as she passed, but Chappell just stared at her and kept going out to the back steps to wait for whatever horrible thing that was going to happen to Lydia to be over.

It took the combined effort of Doc, his wife, and the sheriff to hold Lydia down for the dreadful, degrading, intrusive examination. She was hysterical and fought them like a mountain lion, but in the end they got the information they needed, and then the doctor's wife washed Lydia's pitiful body, redressed her in the torn, dirty dress, and held Lydia in her strong arms until the stricken child had calmed down, putting her to sleep in the little room off the porch reserved for hired help. Meanwhile, Doc furiously wrote down all his findings for the record, and then stuffing everything into his black bag, he gathered his wife and went home, handing his report to the sheriff on his way out.

The sheriff hastily read the report, scowling and shaking his head intermittently, then placed it on the table and headed outside to the second sheriff's car to fetch Earl. Now Earl, Chappell, Darius and the sheriff sat together at the kitchen table gaping at each other, waiting for someone to speak.

"Well, was she…?" Earl started the awkward conversation.

The sheriff shook his head, "Yeah, she's hurt pretty bad, too."

Chappell's lips quivered, but Earl went white with rage.

"Why didn't ya' let me kill the bastard when I had the chance?" he roared, slamming his fist down onto the table, and he jumped up to leave. The sheriff headed him off before he could get out of the kitchen.

"There's other things to decide right now, Earl, so sit down!"

Earl's breathing was heavy, and he shook with emotion, but finally he acquiesced and sat back down.

"He'll go to jail, won't he?" Earl asked.

"God knows he should go to the chair for this, but that means a trial, ya' know? Do ya' really want to put that little girl through the humiliation of a trial?" the sheriff took off his hat and wiped his brow. "Hasn't she been through enough?"

"I want him to pay for what he done to my girl! If that means a trial, so be it!" Earl declared.

"Yeah? Do ya' have money for an expensive attorney, Earl? 'Cause that's what it'll take, a really good attorney to put that son of a .." the sheriff stopped speaking and wiped his mouth with the back of his hand.

"What do we do, then? Just let him go free?"

"No, I can arrest him on other charges. Lydia apparently surprised him at his hidden field in the woods, and he was afraid she would give him away. He has thousands of dollars worth of marijuana in that field, nothin' to sniff at. Anyway, he's goin' away a long time for that."

"That's not good enough!" Earl spit out.

"It's better than dragging yer little girl's reputation through the mud! What respectable man 'round here's gonna' want her for a wife afta' this? You think long and hard on it, Earl. You'll see. It's best just to let it pass," the sheriff admonished.

Chappell had been listening quietly with her eyes downcast, but now she rose slowly and walked towards the small, plain, china hutch. She stopped in front of it, opened a drawer, drew out a large butcher knife, and proceeded to slash the sides of her neck, laughing wildly as the blood gushed out onto her shoulders and soaked the front of her dress.

"Oh my God!" Earl screamed and wrestled the knife away from his wife.

"Grab some towels, boy, sheets, anything you can find!" the sheriff bellowed his orders to Darius, but the young boy was in shock and just stood there gaping at his mother's gushing wounds before passing out cold onto the floor.

Chapter Fourteen

"Lydia! Come out! What're ya' doin' unda' there? You're scaring me! Lydia!" Chappell was tugging at Lydia's leg, trying to rouse her and get her out from under the back steps.

Lydia opened her eyes, slowly comprehending where she was, and began to inch her way from under the stairs. She sat upright on the bare ground, looking at Chappell's confused and anxious face.

"I know," she said feebly, "I remember."

Chappell caught her breath, and then with quivering lips, began to cry, clenching her hands in her lap. Lydia reached out and took her mother's hands.

"I understand," Lydia said softly to her.

"Oh, Lydia, it was such a horrifying day, such a ghastly time. No one knew what to do to make it right, and I ..." she sobbed.

"Sh-sh-sh..." Lydia comforted.

"I abandoned ya'. I abandoned both of ya'. My dear pitiful children, left to fend for themselves. I have neva" forgiven myself, and I have neva' forgiven yer father, either."

"Dad?" What did he do wrong?"

"Mr. Woodall was a parolee, and they're not allowed to have alcohol, but Earl felt sorry for him and gave him liquor from time to time. They would stand right out there at the well and drink it. I neva' trusted that awful man. I just had a feelin' 'bout him, like he's up to no good, but yer father wouldn't listen to me, and kept lettin' him hang 'round. He plowed a field on our land without us knowin', and planted illegal stuff there, and that's where he…" Chappell choked up before she could finish explaining.

"I rememba' comin' 'cross him in the woods, wavin' at him, smilin', but him lookin' at me like he'd seen a ghost. His eyes were terrible under that old dirty hat. I tried to run, but he grabbed me 'round the neck and threw me on the ground and…" Lydia swallowed, "…kept hurtin' me. I fought him hard, but then somethin' bashed me in the head. The last thing I rememba' is feelin' dirt bein' thrown on my face, but not bein' able to move, like I was paralyzed."

"Yer dad was with the sheriff when he found the little grave. Yer blood was all ova' the ground there, and mixed all in the dirt in the grave," Chappell took Lydia's face in her hands, "To this day, no one knows how ya' got outta' that grave, not even Mr. Woodall, but somehow ya' got back home alive."

"It had to be Jesus. It had to be God, 'cause I can't tell ya' how either. I couldn't move and I was so scared that I couldn't keep myself awake. The next thing I knew, I was there at the edge of the yard lookin' for yer face in the kitchen winda', but you weren't there. I know now, you were out lookin' for me."

Tears of release and gratitude poured refreshingly down Lydia's face and she reached to embrace her mother. They held onto each other and cried for a long while before rising to get on with the day. Chappell climbed the steps to go back into the house, but Lydia stood there, hesitantly looking around as if she did not know what to do.

"Lydia?"

"I need to see Dad."

Chappell took a long deep breath and exhaled it slowly.

"He was headed for the tractor shed the last time I saw 'im. Tread softly with 'im, Lydia. He's a broken man. He has been for a long time now."

Lydia shook her head and then proceeded down the path between the wood shed and the pack house to find her father. She prayed as she walked.

"Father, thank ya' for this sweet, sweet gift. Thank ya' for freein' my mind. Now, I've got one more thing to ask of ya', if it won't be too much in one day. Please git my dad's heart ready for me, ya' know? Let him listen to me, and look at me, and really talk with me instead of just, well, fightin' with me. Let us settle it once and for all today."

Lydia heard her father tinkering under the tin hood of the old Ford tractor before she could see him. Looking at the impressive antique machine brought back happy memories of her family when they used to actually farm the land together with Lydia and Darius riding the huge rounded fenders of the massive red tractor. She even remembered them raising a lot of their own food, and having a milk cow, and gathering chicken eggs for breakfast. There were happy family memories to be had. There were happy memories still to be made, and by the grace of her magnificent God, they would do it, but the past had to be buried first before they could step into the future.

Lydia hadn't meant to sneak up on her father; she was just standing there reminiscing when he lowered the folding metal hood and saw her. He jumped back.

"My God! What's the idea spyin' on me when I'm workin'?" he demanded, putting away his hand tools in a quaint old wooden box that had belonged to his father, and to his father before him. He took out a ragged cloth and began wiping the oil and grease from his fingers and palms, looking up at Lydia as if wondering why she was still there. Lydia smiled lovingly at him.

"I'm sorry," she offered faintly.

"What? Oh, well, just don't do it again," her father insisted.

"No, I mean, I'm sorry for all you've been through 'cause of me," she spoke softly, walking around the end of the tractor.

"Stay right there," he ordered stepping back away from her. "What're ya' talkin' 'bout?" he wanted to know. "How would ya' know what I've been through?"

"I don't know all that you've suffa'd, but I do know some. I remema', Dad; I remema' the whole terrible night, and I know how ya' looked everywhere for me, and how ya' were goin' to kill that wretched man on my account." Lydia stepped a little closer to her father. This time he did not move away; he just kept gazing at her like he was seeing her for the first time, but his mood was tenuous, so Lydia stopped where she was.

"How do ya' know all this? Yer mom and I swore we'd neva' talk 'bout that night again. Have ya' been troublin' yer mom 'bout this, cause if ya' have...?"

"No, I didn't have to. I went wanderin' in the woods today, prayin' for God to help me be free from my past, thinkin' 'bout ole' Duke, and came across that hidden field, and well, I guess it just shocked my brain into rememberin', cause the whole sorry mess came floodin' into my head 'fore I could stop it."

Earl backed up and sat down heavily on a tall log stump standing on end under the shed roof. He looked genuinely exhausted, and wiped the sweat and dirt from his face with a handkerchief he always kept in his pocket for that purpose. Then he raised his eyes and looked intently into Lydia's face, lost in thought, the muscles of his own face fluidly shifting from one emotion to another, and then suddenly he smiled.

"You were such a cute little thing then, and full of curiosity. No one could keep ya' still or quiet for very long at a time. Why, you would ask all these head scratchin' questions," he chuckled, "and we'd have to go look up the answers, 'cause we wouldn't know. Why, one time, before we could stop ya', ya' stood up on the pew at church and corrected the preacha's gramma'!" Earl blurted out with nervous laughter.

Lydia giggled, too, "I rememba' that! I also rememba' being soundly whipped afterwards," she grinned.

Earl quit laughing and once again fixed his eyes on Lydia's face.

"You're beautiful like yer mom."

"Thanks," she said, looking down. She felt uneasy and embarrassed at being complemented by this man after so many years of his insults, yet Lydia was grateful for such a restful, normal chat, the kind most fathers and daughters have everyday.

"Dad, I meant what I said earlier. I'm sorry for all those years of sorrow ya' went through on my account. I don't know how to make it up to ya', but I want ya' to please forgive me. Can you do that?"

Earl seemed perplexed by her request. He just stared at her with a frown on his face, shaking his head slowly from side to side.

"Yer mom had gone up the road to take some food to that old lady who lived in that run down one room shack. She left you children with me, and I left you and yer brotha' at the playset at the back of the yard while I went to milk the cow. 'Don't go anywhere', I'd said, 'I'll be right back,' but you grew restless and headed out with yer dog to look for me. Darius was callin' for ya' when I got back. Poor boy was so scared. He and I called for ya' 'til we were blue in the face. Then yer mom got home and insisted on fetchin' the sheriff. She was so angry at me…still is."

"I'm so sorry, Dad. Please forgive me," Lydia cried, her shoulders shaking.

"You were just a tiny, little girl, Lydia. I was the one at fault, wasn't I? That wicked man wouldn't have even been on my property if I hadn't befriended him, and I should've taken you and Darius with me to the pasture. Simple things. I just weren't being careful with my family."

"Dad, I love ya'," his daughter choked out the words through her tears.

"No, Lydia, don't! I don't deserve it! I killed yer dog, girl, 'cause he didn't protect ya'. How can ya' love me for that? How many years now have I made ya' pay miser'bly for my guilt, my sin? Don't say ya' love me. Ya' don't have to go that far, but do say you'll pray for me to yer God, and that you'll ask him to have mercy on me, and save me. Will ya', Lydia? Can ya' do that for me?"

Lydia rushed to her father and flung her arms around him, ignoring his attempts to push her away, until finally, he gave in to her embrace, and enveloped her in his arms. It was a magnificent moment and Lydia could almost hear the enthusiastic approval of God's heavenly host. Earl cleansed his heart of all its bitterness and guilt that afternoon as the blood of Christ flowed through his soul, and he allowed God to commence healing his jaded emotions and be a balm for his torn spirit.

To say that Chappell was surprised when she looked out her kitchen window and saw Earl and his daughter walking hand in hand up the tractor trail from the shed to the house would be a gross understatement. At first, her heart jumped with fear that he was compelling Lydia to walk with him that way, but when Chappell heard the laughter and jovial prattle between them, she was both relieved and extremely curious. What had happened at the tractor shed to cause such a miraculous union? Chappell stepped outside the back door and waved at them. Lydia and Earl both waved back.

"Ain't she beautiful?" Earl asked his daughter.

"I've always thought so," she answered with a smile.

It would now be up to her father to make amends with his wife and grow into the husband and spiritual leader that she needed him to be. He would also have to reconcile with Darius and become an example of manhood of which his son could be proud.

That evening, after everyone had hugged good night and retired to their perspective rooms, Lydia opened her window and gazed up at the moon. There was no need for words that night; the praise of her heart wafted to God on the wings of her spirit, and His spirit met her in the quiet of the stark bedroom where they communed for a long while, and during this spiritual union, God spoke to Lydia's heart, "I have not called you to perform, but to teach and to counsel." This fellowship was like nothing else Lydia had ever known, and she did not want it to end, but soon exhaustion overtook her and she had to say goodnight to her Lord and crawl into bed and sleep, but before she did, she thanked God that she knew.

Chapter Fifteen

"I don't understand, Lydia. This is the chance of a lifetime! Why wouldn't you want to take advantage of it? Were your parents opposed or something? If so, I can talk to them and make them understand how important this is," Mr. Sutton was pacing back and forth in his tiny office with his hands clasped behind his back as he sputtered out his speech.

"My parents left it up to me," Lydia spoke softly. She could understand his disappointment--he had been hoping that the small college could benefit by receiving some of the royalties from the sale of the music--but she had to stand her ground.

"They did? Then I'm doubly baffled!"

"Mr. Sutton, I prayed earnestly for God to guide me in this matter, to let me know without a shadow of a doubt what to do, and He did. Now I have a peace 'bout it, but if ya' don't, well you'll have to take yer own heart before God."

She rose to leave.

"Wait, Lydia, you're right. I know you're right," he scratched his head and then walked over to her. "You will keep singing for the choir when we perform, won't you?"

Lydia grinned, "Sure I will, and you can record it if ya' like," she winked and then headed for the cafeteria.

For the next three years, Lydia sang in the choir during the school year, and on weekends she travelled with small ensembles that toured around the state garnering support for the college, but when she was not traveling in the summers, Lydia was working at the dry cleaners with Mike back home. He always had a job available for her when she was home from college, and now coming home was a pleasure. Each August, Darius joined the family for a couple of weeks before going back to school, and together he and the rest of the family made a horde of great new memories to fill them all year long.

Darius graduated at the end of Lydia's junior year with a degree in computer programming and a minor in business administration. He had already been offered a job with a company in Richmond with which he had done his internship, but he did not want to always be so far from his parents, so he talked to them about moving to the Richmond area, or at least on a farm in the county outside the area, and amazingly, they offered to think about it.

Lydia spent the first part of her senior year praying about where to "teach or counsel" after graduation. Christian schools were springing up plentifully across the eastern coastal states in reaction to the liberal antics of the sixties and seventies, so there were plenty of opportunities to apply for work. However, with each attempt to choose a school at which to apply, her spirit would restlessly resist like a cat being placed into a bath tub full of water, and one application after another would end up crumpled and thrown into the trash.

"What's the problem?" she lamented to her long time roommate, Cindy, after throwing yet another application into the large trash can with which she had replaced her smaller one. "Why can't I bring myself to do this? The school year will end soon, and all the jobs will be taken 'fore I get 'round to applyin'."

Cindy, who had been watching her roommate suffer through applications for a month or two, climbed down off her bunk and sat on the edge of Lydia's desk, holding Lydia's hand in hers.

"I've lived with you for almost 4 years now, and I've watched you grow from an anxious and withdrawn farm girl, who had to sneak out at night and go prowling to survive, into a confident spirit filled woman who had the guts to say 'no' to an offer anyone else would have jumped on with two feet just because God, her father, said He wanted her to do something else. He spoke to you, and you listened, and you just knew. What makes you think that this will be any different?"

Cindy patted her friend's hand and went back to her bunk to read.

Lydia watched her wise roommate walk away, contemplating her words. Cindy was right, as usual, and Lydia pushed herself away from her desk and started dressing for work.

"Ya' knew I was sneakin' out at night?"

"Yep. Almost turned you in once."

"Ya' did? What stopped ya'?"

"You were doing what I wished I'd had the guts to do. Besides, I'd have missed that crazy Virginia accent if they kicked you out," Cindy smiled and turned to finish reading her book.

Lydia headed to the door to leave for work, but then turned around.

"Luv' ya'," she said to her good friend.

"Yeah, me too," Cindy returned without looking up.

As she walked down the walk toward the cafeteria, Lydia thought about those times when she slipped out of the dorm at night, and of the last time when the young boy almost lost his life right in front of her. How had he gotten involved with that criminal element in the first place? What caused teens to fall away from their parents' teaching and get so involved in dangerous things like drugs and crime? Was it the farm upbringing that had kept Darius and her from falling prey to the same thing, or was it the fear they both had for their father? Lydia pondered these things as she walked, occasionally bumping shoulders with students, apologizing for not looking where she was going.

Even at work, the image of the teenage boy in the park haunted Lydia, and she found it hard to focus on what she was serving. Her manager, who by now knew Lydia's work habits very well, came up behind her on the serving line.

"What?" he spoke in her ear.

She jumped, and then laughed, "Man, don't scare me like that!"

"Sorry, but I can tell you're not with us tonight, and I just wondered what huge thing you were thinking about this time? Have you been asked to fly to the moon? Is the president coming here to give you a medal, what?"

She laughed at his sarcastic humor, "Am I not doin' a good job? Sorry, I'll focus betta'. Honest!"

"No, I just want to know what's going on so this time I can be in on the praying. If I had known what a decision you were trying to make the last time, I would have been praying for you, that's all."

Lydia was moved to tears and put down her huge metal serving spoon and hugged her manger's neck.

"That's so sweet. Sure, I'll tell ya' afta' we're done here. Okay?"

He shrugged a yes and went back into the kitchen.

Later, when all the students had gone, and everyone was wiping tables, Lydia's manager came out to the floor, and she told him of the agony through which she was going trying to bring herself to apply for a job at a Christian school, and how frustrating it was to want a job like that but not be able to have peace about it. He listened intently, as did her fellow workers who had finished their tables and had gathered around hers, and then motioned for everyone to sit down. They all huddled around one table, waiting to hear the manger's words as he was very seldom this attentive to anyone, and all were curious to get a glimpse of this man's true personality.

Taking off his large apron, he sat down among his young employees, looking slowly around the table from one face to another until he got to Lydia. His countenance was unsympathetic, but his voice was passionate, and Lydia could tell that he was deeply moved not just by her plight, but for the futures of all the students sitting there. When he spoke, it was with the kind of authority that comes from spending much time in the presence of the Lord.

"God's will is not like a menu, or map, or contract, or any other stupid thing you may have heard from a pulpit. God's will is his character, just look up the Hebrew. It's God's character that you seek, his face, his personality, and his desires not just for you but for his kingdom. How do you seek his face and know his character? You stay in his presence through prayer, lots and lots of prayer, all day long, not in fifteen minutes of so called devotions, and you actually live by what you read in the Bible each day, and if you don't understand what you read, you ask! That's the job of the Holy Spirit that lives in you, to 'teach you all things whatsoever [Christ] has given him,' right? When you became Christians, guys, you may have become part of the church of Christ that meets in a building every Sunday, but you also stepped into a battle for the lost souls of men, and that is your focus and God's will for you—to know Him so well that he can flow through you to the lost wherever you are, whatever you're doing, whether it's teaching, preaching, or working at a service station. It's God's character you want to know. His will is his character, and if you are well acquainted with that, then you'll never need to worry if you're in the will of God or not. Wherever you find yourself, you'll be in His will. Now, you got that?" he looked around at all the faces mesmerized by his words. They shook their heads slowly, and sat there waiting for more like hungry baby birds with their little beaks open. "If you liked that, come back tomorrow night, and we'll talk more," he said and then, slapping his hand down on the table, he added, "Now, let's all go home."

As the crowd was dispersing, Lydia grabbed her manager by the arm.

"Wait, you're really knowledgeable. Why aren't ya' a pastor somewhere or somethin'?" she asked.

He laughed, "I got my theology degree, my master of theology, and half the work done for my doctorate before I woke up one morning and realized how much time I had spent gaining knowledge and how little time I had spent knowing God. Worse, how much time I had lost not winning the lost or discipling young believers. I had lived to myself pretty much all that time, and after I got down on my knees and repented to my Lord for ignoring him all those years, I asked him to put me where he could use me most, and he put me here. Lydia, I've never regretted it. What God has allowed me to do in the lives of young Christians here, and in the lives of the members of my church, and in my own neighborhood has been the most wonderful, rewarding life I could have ever asked for."

He smiled, and placed his hand on Lydia's shoulder.

"You know this already, Lydia. Don't get caught up in the church career mentality. It's not a career you seek, it's service," and with these words, he walked away.

Lydia could not sleep that night thinking of her manager's words which were still burning in her heart. Tossing and turning on her squeaky upper bunk, she felt guilty about keeping her roommate awake and finally climbed down and set off up the hallway to the lounge where she scrunched up her legs under her on the end of a sofa and drew open the blinds to look at the full, bright, somber moon. Feathery, translucent clouds danced lightly across its face like lace over the countenance of a bride, and Lydia smiled remembering another night when she had gazed up at the moon while praying about an impossible decision. Now here she was again, basking in the light of this glowing orb as she thought about all that her cafeteria manager had shared with them tonight. Where was the need? Where was her heart? How could God bring them both together and guide her into a service in which she would be used to the hilt?

"Father, I'm at a loss. It don't matta' to me none what ya' do with me, or where ya' put me, but I gotta' be honest; it does botha' me not to know," she could feel her throat tighten as emotions welled up inside her. "That boy, Lord, what eva' became of that boy? Is he alive or dead? Should I have helped him more? Could I have helped him more without getting us both killed?" she shifted in her seat and grabbed a pillow to put under her arms, and then sat quietly waiting for some response.

"Ya' know, Lord, I coulda' been him, if ya' hadn't found me. There's prob'bly a million of us out there right now--hurt, angry, and bitta. If it hadn't been for Mrs. Lorraine gettin' involved with my mom, I wouldn't be here now. She's like my managa', isn't she? Right in the middle of yer will for her life, savin' souls, nursing young believers, though she ain't actually paid by a school or church. I want that, Lord. I want to be used like that."

Lydia allowed her tears to spill over her cheeks and fall unimpeded down her face as she knelt next to the sofa in the moonlight and prayed to be used.

"I'll go whereva' ya' want me to go, and do whateva' ya want me to do, just use me, Lord. Use me!"

Lydia stayed on her knees there by the sofa waiting on the Lord until sleepiness overcame her and she trodded softly back down the hallway to her room, climbing as quietly as possible back into her bunk to await the sunrise.

Chapter Sixteen

It was hard getting out of bed the next morning, but Lydia dragged herself up and before long was headed to the bookstore where she would work until her first class began. She deliberately avoided any thoughts about the future, and just enjoyed the moment in which she found herself, waiting on her friends, and organizing the merchandise for which she was responsible. There was a lot of excited talk about spring break which would be upon them in a couple of weeks, and Lydia found herself longing for home, but she would be on her last tour with the choir during break, so a visit home would have to wait until after graduation. Darius and her parents were already writing her asking about her plans for the summer, and if she had a job come fall, but she had not written them back because she did not want to alarm them by having no prospects yet. She would know soon. She would just know.

A group of students was organizing a trip to a neighborhood in another part of town in order to hand out tracts door to door and asked Lydia if she wanted to go along. This type of activity was not usually of interest to Lydia as she was somewhat shy talking to strangers, but today she felt compelled to go with them, and so boarded the large van with a packet of tracts in her hand.

The neighborhood was not too far away from the college which was actually in a rather questionable part of town to begin with, so they did not travel far before getting out among lower middle class houses obviously inhabited by people without the money to keep up appearances, or perhaps without the initiative for whatever reason. The students divided themselves into four groups of three people for safety reasons, and then spread out along the street going in opposite directions away from the site of the van. There was nothing about these houses or this neighborhood that made Lydia feel uncomfortable--she had grown up in worse than this--but the hard glares that she got from the people who answered the doors distressed her a bit, and she began to feel like an interloper. What was she doing here? She would probably never see these people again, and the people knew it, and they understood that the students were just fulfilling some requisite to witness and do their duty to God, but that they were not really there to help them with real needs. Many of the people were out of work because of the recession, and many more had jobs that paid less than the work justified. Lydia felt foolish and embarrassed and found herself apologizing for intruding on their lives.

She was relieved when they finally arrived at the last house on their side of the street. They ascended the porch stairs and noticed that the screen door was hanging by one hinge against the wall beside the door, and bags of empty liquor bottles were piled up on the porch inviting flies. One of the girls put up her hand to wrap the door with her knuckles, but then hesitated.

"I'm not sure about this one, guys. Maybe we should go?" she whispered, but about that time, the splintered wooden front door flew open.

"What do ya' want!" asked a slurred, gruff voice from inside. The two girls with Lydia jumped back startled and turned to run down the steps, but Lydia was frozen to the spot. The voice took her back to her childhood, and her instincts were to freeze so as not to be detected. In a moment, however, she came to herself, but not in time to leave before the brusque man appeared at the door holding one of his liquor bottles and wreaking of whiskey. Lydia stared speechlessly at the crusty, bearded man with scars on his face.

"Well, what is it?" he asked squinting at the sun streaming into his front door silhouetting her tall slender figure. "Can I help ya'?"

Lydia glanced at the seemingly useless tract in her hand, and then looked back at the scary man. Would he even read it, or just throw it in the trash?

"Sir, I have somethin' I would like for ya' to read..."

"Where're ya' from, girl?" he asked oblivious to the tract she was holding out to him.

"I'm from Virginia, sir,"

"What part?" he seemed agitated.

"The southern part, sir. Why do ya' ask?" she was curious now and tired of a stranger asking her personal questions. About that time, a teenaged boy appeared behind the man looking over his shoulder to see what Lydia had in her hand. She gasped and pointed wide-eyed at the boy.

"You!" she blurted out.

The gruff man turned and glared at his son in anger.

"What have ya' done now, ya' fool," he turned back around to face Lydia. "Has he done somethin' to ya' girl? I wanna' know if he has!"

"Oh, no, sir, I just saw him once a few years ago, and well, I was surprised to run into him again, that's all," she stammered never taking her eyes off the boy who appeared to be about sixteen years old now.

He stepped out from around his father and onto the porch where he eyeballed Lydia up and down with a frowning countenance.

"I don't rememba' yer face none," he said glaring at her suspiciously.

"Well, ya' wouldn't. Ya' neva' saw my face, I just saw yers..." she hesitated, then added, "...in the park that night," she finished, wondering if she had said too much in front of his father.

At first the boy seemed puzzled and shook his head, but then his eyes widened, and he was about to say something, but remembering that his dad was still standing there, he closed his mouth and reached for the tract in Lydia's hand.

"I'll take that," he said, then turned the small tract over in his hand until he found the name of the college and its address stamped at the bottom of the last tiny page. "Yeah, thanks," he said holding the tract up and waving it, "I'll be sure to hang on to this," he said again winking at Lydia.

Lydia told the boy and his strange father goodbye. She knew it would not be the last time that she would see the boy, and she went happily back down the street to the van where the others were waiting for her with abated breath hoping she was safe. While the others chattered away endlessly on the ride back to school, Lydia watched out the window at all the houses passing by and wondered how many more people like the boy and his father lived in these neighborhoods. They needed to be saved and belong to God, but what did they need to bring them to the point where they would be willing to listen to her tell about their need to be saved? Lydia felt a longing stirring in her to reach these neighborhoods of people for Christ, but how would she do it? Where could she start?

That night at dinner, Lydia shared her burden for the people with her beloved friend and roommate, Cindy, who listened intently and then began to offer brilliant suggestions about how Lydia could begin a ministry like the one she envisioned.

"…and I'll help you," she concluded after rattling off a list of ideas which Lydia furiously wrote down.

"You will? Oh, that would be so wonderful! Thanks, Cindy," she said.

"Why do you think that horrible man wanted to know where you were from?" Cindy asked.

"I don't know, but there was somethin' about him that made my skin crawl; somethin', well, almost sinister," she shivered, "Maybe it was the way he talked? I don't know, but it was just weird."

They began the next day to put some of their plans to into action by getting the manager's permission to place large cardboard boxes along an out of the way wall in the cafeteria in which people could put all their unwanted clothing, cans or boxes of food, powdered milk, and other items to be taken out to the neighborhoods and distributed to whomever needed it. Next, they begged permission from the Dean of Women to allow just the two of them to go together in Cindy's car and ask around the neighborhood for someone willing to allow them to use their porch once a week to distribute the items. Finally, they advertised on posters in the hallways of the school for anyone who would like to take part in this ministry to meet Lydia and Cindy in the parking lot of the cafeteria and be ready to load boxes into their cars.

Before bringing the boxes of goods to the neighborhoods, Lydia, Cindy, and the other involved students first handed out fliers to the people explaining where and when they would be in their particular neighborhood. So far, everything was going well, and

Lydia was excited at the prospect of meeting the people on a different level, and she prayed that God would use this ministry to open doors of opportunity to really share the Gospel.

Lydia was on her way to class on a Monday morning when she saw a familiar figure leaning against the brick exterior of the academic building with his hands in his pockets, chewing on the end of a thin reed. He looked around self-consciously, watching the students as they filed through the double glass doors on their way to class, but when he saw Lydia, he waved. Trotting over to her, he asked if he could carry her books.

"Thanks, but I'm goin' right in here, so I'll just hang on to 'em. What're ya' doin' here?" she asked pulling him out of the stream of human traffic to stand in the grass.

"I wanted to thank ya'," he began, "for the park thing. I guess ya' saved my life or somethin'."

Lydia blushed when she smiled, "I didn't do it on purpose, ya' know. I just screamed out when…"

"Well, whatever. I'm still here as a result of it, and well, I wanted to say thanks," he grinned. "What were ya' doin' in the park that night anyway?"

"Just gettin' used to college," she laughed, then added looking at her watch, "speakin' of which, I'm goin' to be late for class. We'll be in your neighborhood on Thursday. Will ya' be there?"

"What time?"

"Around 3:30pm, after classes."

"Yeah, I'll be there," he grinned again, and headed down the street toward town.

Lydia watched him saunter away. She did not know his name, but there was something familiar in his demeanor--though she could not quite put a finger on it--something in his walk or in the look in his eyes that made her uneasy around him. She shook her head and went to class.

On Thursday, Cindy, Lydia, and the others in the ministry, that had affectionately been dubbed "neighborhood reach," showed up to unload boxes of clothes and food at the home of Miss Nellie, an elderly German lady who willingly volunteered her porch as a distribution point for this ministry of which she wanted to be a part. Miss Nellie hugged the girls and others and began to show them where they could place their boxes for the afternoon, informing the volunteers that she had fruit drink and donuts for them inside her kitchen.

On this first trip, only a trickle of people came for assistance, and Lydia was disappointed that the boy from the park did not show up, but on the next visit to this neighborhood, a couple of lines had to be formed to accommodate all the recipients, and the boy from the park not only showed up, he helped disperse items to his neighbors who all seemed to know him and regard him with affection. When the last family had been accommodated, and the team was packing up the empty boxes, Lydia found the boy and shook his hand.

"Thank you so much for yer help. All these people seemed much more comfortable dealing with you than with us, but maybe now, they'll trust us a little more," she said still shaking his hand.

"Hey, any time," he shrugged his shoulders and looked away.

"What's yer name?" Lydia finally asked.

"Tommy," he said frowning at her, and then asked suspiciously, "Why?"

Lydia laughed at him

"So I can turn ya' in to the FBI," she said mockingly.

He laughed and relaxed again, "What's yers?"

"Lydia," she answered.

He quit smiling and looked steadily into her face, searching her features until she began to feel uneasy. There it was again, that hard, treacherous look in his eyes, and Lydia wanted to flee the porch to get out from under his gaze. She turned to leave, but he seized her arm and turned Lydia around to face him.

"How old are ya'?" he demanded glaring at her.

"Why?" she insisted.

"Just tell me, damn it!"

Lydia jerked her arm out of his control, and turned to leave. Cindy had heard the raised voices and was on her way to rescue

Lydia with a couple of guys from the ministry, when Lydia walked by her.

"Don't worry 'bout it. It's ova'. Everything's okay," she said looking back at Tommy before leaving with her friends to get in the van.

"What was that all about?" Cindy wanted to know, "Did he hurt you?"

Lydia examined her arm, but there were only a few red bruises.

"No, I'm fine…thanks…" but then uninvited tears cascaded down her face, and she sobbed on her friend's shoulder all the way back to the college, unloading the familiar aftermath of terror that had been released in her by the incident and the tremendous relief that followed her rescue.

It took a lot of persistence and quick witted arguments to convince the Dean of Women that the ministry was not dangerous and to allow them to try it a little longer, but finally she conceded, and because of the close call with Lydia, more students became involved with Neighborhood Reach if for no other reason than the fact that there is strength in numbers. It didn't matter to Lydia what the reasons were; she was just delighted that there would be so many students to take over the ministry after she and Cindy graduated that spring.

Thursday each week was the official day to deliver aid through Neighborhood Reach, and more and more people came to receive the beneficial goods and to stay and listen to the testimonies of the students. Before long, there were several new believers, and a Bible study was formed to disciple these newborn Christians whose numbers grew each week as they testified to one another in their neighborhood leading their friends and relatives to the Lord.

Lydia could not thank God enough for what He was doing among these people, but her heart ached that neither the young boy, nor his father ever came back to get food or clothing, neither did they come out to hear the testimonies. She felt guilty for treating the son the way she had on the porch, and prayed for God to give her another chance with the boy, but week after week, he did not show up.

Much time passed, and now graduation was just around the corner, and all the seniors were busy finishing up treatises, ordering graduation caps and gowns, buying tassels, and signing year books, so Lydia did not have a lot of time to think about the boy or his father. However, she did think about Miss Nellie one busy day, and decided to ask Cindy to go with her to the old lady's house to thank her for taking a chance on two crazy girls with boxes and a dream, so they set out that very afternoon bearing flowers for their elderly friend.

Miss Nellie was on her porch as usual on that sunny afternoon, and the girls hugged her as she greeted them with surprise. They presented her with the flowers which she insisted on promptly placing in water in a beautiful antique glass vase that had belonged to her saintly mother. The group of friends sat and talked for a good little while on the spacious front porch, and Lydia realized how much she was going to miss her college, this ministry, and especially her beloved friends, and she could not help but cry, but she did not cry alone. The whole group locked arms and cried tears of joy over what God had wrought in their lives together and tears of sadness over the rapidly approaching separation.

After a few minutes, Lydia excused herself from her friends' embraces and walked up the street to Tommy's house not knowing for sure why she was going there, only that she felt compelled to go. She walked tentatively up the steps and was poised to knock on the door when it opened slowly and Tommy appeared.

"Yeah?" he asked, his expression rigid.

Lydia could not speak at first. She was still choked up from earlier emotions that were still very near the surface.

"I came to say that I'm sorry for, well, for walkin' away from ya' on the porch...uh, ya' know...weeks ago. Ya' just scared me, that's all," she said softly.

Tommy looked at her for a few moments, then sighing he smiled, melting away his hard countenance.

"Heck, I only wanted to know how old ya' are," he grinned.

"I'm 21. Be 22 in August," she answered wondering why it was so important to him. She was far too old for him to be interested in her, so what could be his reason for being so adamant to know that day on the porch.

Tommy looked down shaking his head in satisfaction, but Lydia could see that his brain was calculating something, and the hair on the back of her neck stood up, a warning that all was not well. She had felt the sensation once before long ago.

"Wait here for a minute, will ya'?" he asked. ·

He disappeared into the house closing the door behind him and left Lydia alone on the porch. In a few minutes he was back, smiling, and motioned with his hand for her to have a seat on the porch. Lydia looked around tentatively for a porch rocker without a bag of empty smelly liquor bottles in it in which to sit, but could not find one.

"Oh, sorry," Tommy apologized and cleared off a rocker for her.

"Thank you," she said and sat down. He sat opposite her on the porch rail and seemed to want to talk, but did not know how to start.

"Where did ya' say you were from?" he began.

"Virginia."

"Oh, yeah, that's right," he grinned and then began to pick at a tiny fleck of peeling paint on the porch post next to which he sat.

"Cluster Springs, Virginia," she added, "My folks still live there, but my brotha' lives in Richmond," she volunteered, but then wished she had not given him so much information about herself. He was still a stranger after all.

He shook his head in approval, and then fell silent again messing with an ant crawling towards him on the rail whose paint was badly blistered. After a few more awkward moments, Lydia decided to say goodbye and join her friends again, but she wanted to give him a tract before she left and to encourage him to call the number on the tract if he decided to give his heart to the Lord and wanted someone to help him.

"Tommy, would ya' mind if I gave ya' another tract? It's differ'nt than the other one I gave ya' a while back. I think you'll like it…" she said, and handed it out to him hoping he would take it.

He looked down at the tract, and then fixed his gaze mischievously on Lydia.

"I'll take the tract if ya' also give me an invitation to yer graduation," he bargained grinning.

"Really? Ya' want to sit through a graduation of someone ya' don't even know?"

"Well, I'd wouldn't call the person who saved my life someone I hardly know," he said so sincerely that Lydia's throat tightened, and it was all she could do not to throw her arms around his neck and hug him.

"Well, I don't have one with me," she thought a moment. "Ya' know where ya' met me at school a few months back, in front of the academic building?"

"Yeah," he answered.

"Meet me there again in the next day or so, and I'll have one for ya'. Come the same time ya' did before, hear?" she waited for a reply.

"I'll be there," he promised.

They said their goodbyes and Lydia went back up the street to meet her friend and head back to school. This had been a profitable trip after all, and Lydia prayed for the boy's salvation all the way to the dorm.

Chapter Seventeen

"Do you know yet where you'll be teaching next fall?" her advisor wanted to know. It was Lydia's final session with her, and was supposed to be used to wrap up final details of a new job after graduation, but in this case, the session threatened to be useless.

"No, ma'am, not yet," Lydia reluctantly admitted.

"Do you not think this is cutting it a little close?" her advisor leaned back in her chair studying Lydia as she spoke.

"Yes, ma'am, but God hasn't told me yet…" she tried to explain, but was cut short.

"God often speaks through the bulletin board full of job openings, Lydia, which are still posted and are not all filled as yet, so there's no excuse for you not to have employment at this point, is there?" her advisor looked at Lydia from over the top of her reading glasses. She then began to examine the list of teaching positions still available, finally choosing one for which she thought Lydia would be well suited.

"Ma'am, I ain't movin' 'til God moves me," Lydia said somewhat defiantly. She was tired of the insinuations of this well-meaning, but clueless, advisor, and she wasn't about to be pushed into a job that she did not feel God wanted her to do.

"I'm only trying to help you, Lydia. I know the financial circumstances under which your family exists, and the strenuous work schedule you have endured for the past four years just to pay your way through school, and I just thought you would be happy to finally have an income that was above poverty level doing something that you really enjoyed," the kind hearted advisor said laying her hand over Lydia's. Lydia felt remorse for the brusque way in which she had addressed the advisor.

"I'm sorry, ma'am, I didn't mean to be ugly to ya', but I have to let God lead me in the way that He always has before, or I can't be sure it's really Him leadin', ya' know?

The advisor leaned back in her chair again, taking off her glasses.

"I understand, I think," she conceded.

"I promise ya' that if I don't know by graduation day, I'll come in here the very next mornin', and I'll let ya' put me whereva' ya' think God wants me. Deal?" Lydia stuck out her hand.

"Promise?" the advisor asked with her head tilted to one side.

"Promise."

"It's a deal, and Lydia, I'll pray that God does let you know by then, okay?"

"Thank ya' so much," Lydia said and came around the desk to hug her advisor before leaving the office.

Tommy came by that day to get his graduation invitation. Lydia still thought it strange that he wanted to come, but she wasn't about to talk him out of it when she knew that he would hear about Jesus and salvation during the course of the speeches, so she gave him two invitations and encouraged him to bring his father, too, though she could not see his father bothering to come. Tommy seemed genuinely excited by this turn of events and thanked her profusely. Strange world, she thought.

The school chapel was across the street from the little college, and Lydia was headed that way to graduation practice when she saw that the traffic at the light was backed up in both directions as far as she could see, and sitting there, full of what appeared to be high school students, was a yellow bus broken down and blocking traffic. Another yellow bus was on its way to retrieve the children, but in the meantime, the police would not let any cars or people go by the bus, so Lydia had to wait there at the corner. Some of the young men on the bus were gathered at a couple of windows trying to get her attention.

"Hey!" they yelled, "Hey! You! You a teacher?" they asked Lydia who by now was blushing from the unwanted attention. She remembered the jeering boys at her high school and felt a bit uncomfortable in this situation. Her first inclination was to avoid them, but then she remembered that she was not a teen any more; she was an adult and soon to be a college graduate. Of what did she have to be ashamed?

"I'm goin' to be," she yelled back to the laughing boys.

"Wow, you can teach me anything, anytime!" yelled one handsome boy and his friends joined him in the offer, laughing, enjoying her embarrassment.

Lydia was forced to stand there waiting, so she decided to ignore the loud boys and began perusing the faces in the rest of the bus. There they were, the preppy girls, whispering to each other, talking rapidly and stylishly while the studious students busied themselves with homework. Nothing had changed since she had been in high school. Teens everywhere were the same. Still studying the faces on the bus, Lydia noticed a girl sitting all alone in the very first seat, the one right behind the bus driver. She wasn't talking to anyone, just gazing out the window on the other side of the bus, her chin propped in her hand. Lydia moved down closer to the open door so she could see the girl better. The girl must have sensed Lydia's presence because she turned around, and Lydia gasped. For a horrible moment, she saw herself staring back at her, but then the girl smiled feebly and half lifted her hand in an attempt to wave without being embarrassed if this woman wasn't really looking at her after all. Lydia's heart broke for the girl, and with teary eyes, she smiled and waved back at the girl, and in that moment, Lydia knew without a shadow of a doubt what God wanted her to do after graduation.

"Ma'am, excuse me, can you step back and allow us to unload this bus?" the policeman interrupted Lydia's reverie.

"Oh, certainly!" she moved out of the way and watched as the hyper teens came tumbling down the steps of the bus excitedly talking and totally self-absorbed. The handsome teen boy that had made her an offer grinned as he passed her.

"Offer still stands!" he said and kept on walking.

Lydia smiled when the last girl got off the bus, the one who had sat all alone in the seat behind the driver. She handed her a tract about Jesus that she had in her pocket.

"Take care," she said to the girl who glanced questionably at the tract at first, but then looked back at Lydia smiling. The girl waved timidly at Lydia as she went around the corner of the bus. Lydia stood there silently praising and worshiping God while all around her was the noise of bustling, congested traffic and the honking of impatient drivers. Finally, as the last car passed, Lydia crossed the street feeling as if she was walking on air, gloriously happy that once again she just knew.

Graduation day seemed to arrive without warning, though it could easily be seen on the calendar. All the lists of things that needed to be done by graduation day became the lists of last minute things that had to be done before the actual commencement exercises began. Lydia and her friends were hurrying here and there taking care of exhaustive details from early in the morning until the 1:00pm hour of the graduation, and now it was time to head over to the auditorium basement and line up, but Lydia had one more stop to make first.

In the academic building, along the main hallway, was a wall of tiny mailboxes with minuscule combination locks built into them. Lydia had checked her mailbox every day, rain or shine, since her first day at the college. It had been her lifeline to her mother and brother for the last four years, and a connection to her boss from the dry cleaners, Mike, who had occasionally sent cards to her, so it only seemed right to check it one more time before leaving the institution for good. Lydia was heading up the walkway to the building when she heard a familiar voice calling to her from a short distance. It was Tommy, and he was sprinting across the parking lot toward her, dressed in what was probably his nicest shirt and pants, waving his hand to get her attention.

"Lydia! Wait up!" he called, still sprinting until he was standing in front of her out of breath.

"Hi, Tommy! You're really goin' to see me graduate, aren't ya'?"

"Not just me, my dad's in the car. Come on. Ya'll never really met each otha', and he's waitin' for me to bring ya' ova'," Tommy beamed.

Lydia was hesitant to waste any more time than was necessary, and wasn't sure about going off to the parking lot with two men she hardly knew, but she could see Tommy's dad getting out of the car to meet them, so she shrugged her shoulders and agreed to go.

"Okay, but let's make it quick 'cause I gotta' get in line to walk," she complied.

Tommy followed her into the parking lot as his dad began to walk toward them, placing his old, gray, felt hat on his head, and straightening his waistband. When Lydia saw his hat and the way he was walking, she stopped in her tracks. Her chest grew tight, and she could not breathe. Beads of perspiration popped out on her forehead, and her legs began to shake. As she turned to run, Tommy grabbed her arm and twisted it behind her back, clasping his hand over her mouth before she could scream, though Lydia was too terror stricken to utter a sound.

"Take her inside, boy, quick!" the gruff man ordered.

Tommy dragged Lydia upright into the academic building with his father following close behind. Inside the hallway, the two men glanced around for a place to conceal their actions.

"In here, boy, hurry up!" he again ordered and helped the boy peel Lydia's hand off the door frame. After clearing the opening of the empty dark classroom, the old man closed the door and turned on one of the lights. It was then that Tommy removed his hand from Lydia's mouth, but not his grip of her arm.

"Listen, Lydia, don't scream! We're not here to hurt ya'," he spoke with his mouth close to her ear. "Now, don't scream or run, and I'll let go of yer arm."

Lydia shook her head in agreement, but when he loosed her arm, she shot away a good distance from them and stood against the back wall wishing they were not between her and the door. The old gruff man sat down on one of the desk tops and removed his hat, holding it in his hand. Tommy stood like a sentinel with his arms folded across his chest and a frown on his face.

"What do ya' want?" her voice was faint and cracked, and she was clearly fighting to keep from shaking uncontrollably .

"I didn't know any otha' way to do this, girl. I just had to see ya' and I knew ya'd neva' agree to talk with me if ya' knew who I was. I just wanted to talk to ya', that's all," the old man said wheezing for air.

Tommy looked at his father and then at Lydia, "My dad went to prison when I was four. You put him there," he announced.

Lydia wanted to say that his father deserved to die instead of just going to prison for a few years, but couldn't bring herself to hurt this boy that way, and she was sure that Tommy knew nothing about the rape.

"Now, boy, don't go accusin' this young lady. I went to prison on charges not related to her; she just stumbled onto my stash, that's all. What I did to her, I shoulda' gone to the chair for," said Mr. Woodall shaking his head.

"What're ya' sayin', Dad? I thought we were here for an apology--you know, to make her say she's sorry for what she did to ya'," Tommy argued with his dad.

"No, son, we're here for me to apologize to this young lady," the old man said meekly, "Ya' see, I hurt her real bad, and she won't nothin' but a baby, just a little girl," his voice quivered and he began to choke up with tears. "I read yer tracts, girl. I read how I could be forgiven by Jesus for all my sins and even the sin I did against you. Is that so?"

Tommy looked strangely at his father, "Are ya' tellin' me that ya' raped a child? Her?" he asked incredulously shaking his head.

"I'm so ashamed, son, I'm so ashamed! It was all I could think about for twelve years of prison, and I swore if ever the chance offered itself that I'd make it right, but when we moved away from there, I figured it would neva' happen. And then one day she walks right up to my door! And all I've been able to think about since is gettin' her to forgive me."

"Why didn't ya' tell me this before?" Tommy demanded. "All this time, I thought you were drinkin' yerself to death 'cause of spendin' time in jail, when all the time, it was guilt ova' somethin' wicked ya' did to this girl. I've hated her all this time, and now I find out it's you I should've been hatin'. You bastard!" Tommy lashed out at his father raising his fist.

"Stop!" Lydia screamed afraid that Tommy would hit the old man. "Please stop, both of ya'," she cried and began walking slowly over to her enemies. She put her hand on Tommy's arm lowering his poised fist, and then placed her hand on Mr. Woodall's shoulder, gazing down at the floor for a long moment before speaking.

"I don't even know how to tell ya' the damage ya' did to my family, sir. I can't begin to explain how my life was devastated by yer act in those woods," she began to tremble with passion as she spoke, "and I can't tell ya' how much hate I've held in my heart ova' the years as a result of ya', but God came to me and washed away my shame and hate. He healed me of the wounds and made me his child, ya' hear? I am a child of Almighty God, so the past don't matter any more. I was born all over again at sixteen years old when I saw the face of God and He told me that I was His, and I've been His eva' since," Lydia continued to keep her hand on the old man's shoulder and her hand on Tommy's arm. "I neva' thought I'd see the day when my God would put me here, right in front of the man that destroyed my life, and ask me to forgive 'im."

Mr. Woodall lowered his head and wept loudly, reaching for Lydia's hand. Tommy turned and sat down at a desk with his face in his hands, tears of confusion running down his cheeks. Suddenly, the door to the room burst open and in rushed Earl and Darius. In an instant, Earl had the old man by the collar of his shirt ready to bash in the man's already scarred face. Tommy was in the ominous clutches of Lydia's strong and angry brother.

"Dad, no!" screamed Lydia, "Wait! It's not what ya' think?"

Earl looked puzzled, but slowly released the man as Lydia pulled on his fists to let go. Darius likewise released his prisoner, and all the men stood looking awkwardly at each other.

"Yer roommate said that you'd headed this way. The graduation's getting' ready to start without ya', so we came lookin' for ya'," her father explained, "and when we heard voices, well, we thought you were in trouble."

Earl was studying the face of the old man as he spoke trying to remember from where he knew him, and then he saw his hat which had fallen to the floor in the scuffle, and his face grew white with rage.

"You!" he roared and drew back again to pound the man to oblivion, but Lydia threw herself between them, weeping, and would not let go of the horrible man so her father could take out his long overdue rage on him.

"Lydia, get out of the way!"

"No, Dad! This ain't the way! This ain't God's way!" she pleaded on behalf of the old man.

"It's my way! This is the man that hurt ya', Lydia, and I ain't letting him get away again!" Earl bellowed and tried to pry Lydia away from his foe, but she held on fast.

"He's asking my forgiveness, Dad, my forgiveness," she explained still holding onto the man.

"He's what…" her father said incredulously.

"Asking forgiveness," Darius answered for Lydia walking over to his father and placing his hand on his shoulder, "and it's 'bout time, don't ya' think?"

Lydia's father slowly lowered his arm and let go of the poor scared man so Lydia could at last relax, but then she noticed Tommy was visibly shaken at the violence displayed toward his father, and she wrapped her arms around his shoulders.

"I do, sir...I forgive ya'. There ain't really no other choice when Jesus loves ya' as much as He loves me. How can I do any differ'nt?" she asked quietly.

"I just want to be whole again," sobbed the repentant man, "I just want to have a life and to be used for somethin' good for a change."

Lydia got on her knees in front of the man and pulled him down on his knees beside her, and together they prayed for the salvation of Mr. Woodall, the instrument of destruction to the Marshall family, but now an instrument of edification to the Lord Jesus, and even Tommy slid on his knees and silently prayed next to his father. It was as if the Lord himself was there as a balm of healing from the mercy seat of God poured over the people in this odd tabernacle, and the prayers of worship and praise that were offered up became an especially sweet savory offering in the nostrils of God. It took the sound of processional music to break up this session of adoration, and as Lydia and her father and brother rushed to get Lydia into her place in line, Tommy and his father hurried to find a place to sit and watch.

"Yer mom ain't goin' to understand this none, ya' know," Earl said to Lydia as they darted across the campus to the auditorium, and they all three laughed with exhilaration and relief.

The graduation was wrought with Scripture filled messages and testimonies and the Holy Spirit himself seemed to appear as key note speaker behind every participant. Lydia was so overwhelmed with emotion that when it was time for her to sing one of her songs, by special vote of the senior student body, she was afraid that she would not be able to do it. Nevertheless, she ascended the stage, removing her hat to be able to put the strap of her guitar over her shoulder, and, sitting on a stool, began to sing from the love in her heart for her God:

"My Jesus, I'm not worthy of the nail scars in your hands.
How can I e'er repay you, for the life you gave to man?
My Jesus, I love you; my Jesus, I need you,
To love me, to guide me, to stay always beside me.
Thank you for eternal life, and the promise of your love.
Your love…Your love…Your love."

Chapter Eighteen

It was brisk that morning with sparkling streams of sun seeping into her bedroom window through the kitchen towels that were hung as curtains. Lydia opened her eyes and looked around before rising to meet the day. She had taken over the little bedroom off the side porch, the one reserved for hired hands, and made it her own little haven with pictures on a bulletin board of all her friends from college, a stand for her guitar, and lots of wonderful books, and as she gazed around her tiny room, one picture stood out from all the rest to which she blew a kiss before commencing to dress.

Darius had been offered a job in South Boston that summer and had asked if he could move back into the family home until he could build himself a house on the property. Of course, both Chappell and Earl were ecstatic to have their son home again and to know that he would be settling right there on the farm. Lydia had moved out of their shared bedroom so that he could have it as a place of his own as she would not be there for long.

"Lydia, hurry up! He'll be here soon," Chappell called to her daughter as she fried eggs and sausage on the large, black, cast iron frying pan. Lydia's father had gone out to chop wood for the old cook stove, but now was coming into the back porch with a huge arm load of wood.

"I can see his car turning in now," he declared as he unloaded the wood into the wood box on the porch.

Lydia sat down at the table and gulped down as many bites of food as she could, but her nervousness made it hard to choke down much, so she put an egg in a biscuit and wrapped it in a cloth napkin from the hutch.

"I'll just take it with me and eat it later," she said, gathering her things to go. "Thanks, Mom, for the breakfast," she added kissing her mother on the cheek.

"Good luck at school, Lydia. I still can't believe you're goin' back to yer old high school as a teacher. It's all so wonderful," she said dabbing her teary eyes with the bottom corner of her apron. "I thought we'd loose ya' to some job out a' state like we did yer brother."

"Well, God wanted me here, so that's where I am," she said confidently.

There was a knock on the back screen door, and without waiting for an invitation, a tall handsome young man entered.

"Ready, Miss Teacher?" he said jovially.

Lydia kissed him on the cheek.

"Ready to be Mrs. Teacher soon," she answered.

"Oh, don't I know it!" Mike grinned. "It won't be long now."

Lydia had worked at the dry cleaners as usual that summer while waiting for her new teaching position to begin in the fall.

Before the end of the summer, Mike had asked her to marry him, and though they had never dated, she had said yes because she just knew it was right.

The two lovers jostled up the rutted drive onto the state road and headed toward the high school from which Lydia and her brother had graduated. It was a beautiful sunny late summer day, and except for the tremendous nervousness she felt, Lydia was very happy with her life at that moment and prayed for God to help her get through this first day of school in tact and without panicking. Mike held her hand while they drove along.

"Don't worry. You're the boss now, not the student," he said laughingly. "They can't hurt ya'."

Lydia smiled at this dear sweet man who never ceased to be a testimony to her of hard work, good morals, and genuine concern for the things of God. He had always been such a hero to her of sorts, from the day he first hired her to the day he asked her to marry him. There was just something very trustworthy and faithful about him, and Lydia had grown to love and trust him over the years like nobody else she knew.

Mike dropped Lydia off at the front entrance to the school. She was there earlier than required in order to have more time to prepare her classroom for her students. She entered the dark building, her steps echoing in the East wing as she clip-clopped along in her semi-high heels, and everywhere along the route to her room, ghosts from her past reenacted scenes of prejudice and chauvinism. For one brief painful moment David drifted like a specter across her mental vision, lingering at her locker, straightening his preppy clothes, running his fingers through his perfect hair. Lydia shuddered and stopped there in the hallway, frozen with doubt and apprehension. What was she doing here? Her throat began to ache as it tightened, and tears brimmed her eyes.

Suddenly, Lydia heard the heavy double steel doors open at the end of the hallway, and she whirled around to see the outline of a man coming towards her. As his heavy footsteps ricocheted around her, fear enveloped her and she instinctively turned to take off quickly in the opposite direction, but before she could move, the man called out to her.

"Lydia!" bellowed the welcomed voice of her brother, "Wait up!"

"Darius!" she answered and her legs went weak with relief.

She was about to hug her brother when Darius handed his sister a bouquet of wildflowers in a beautiful glass vase. She laughed and hugged the bouquet to her chest smelling the aroma of the fresh cut flowers.

"How sweet! And they're so beautiful," she gushed.

"I knew how hard it would be for ya' to be in this place again, and well, I wanted ya' to know that you're goin' to do okay. I just know it. So ever'time you're feelin' panicky, just look at those flow'rs and remember I'm here with ya'," her brother encouraged her.

Lydia threw her arms around his neck and hugged him tight.

"Thanks, Darius. You'll neva' know how much this means to me right now," she said gratefully. Lydia and Darius continued up the hallway to Lydia's classroom where she would be teaching algebra and geometry, her favorite maths. The flowers were placed lovingly in a vase and set on her desk at the front of the room, and then she opened the blinds to let in the beautiful sunshine.

"Well, you're here now, so I'll be heading to work. God bless ya', Lydia. God bless everything ya' think, everything ya' say, and everything ya' do," Darius exalted her and then left her there in the peacefulness of the empty classroom.

Lydia prayed watching through the window as the first bus arrive and rambunctious students poured out its door clad in all the latest fashions, carrying the most popular styled book bags, displaying impeccable hairstyles, and sporting more than adequate shoes.

"God, I need ya'. Let me know who's hurtin', and who needs to be protected, and who needs to be awakened to what they're doin' that's wrong, but also give me a love and concern for all the students no matta' how rotten their attitudes are. Oh, and help me be strong but compassionate in front of these guys, and for all this, I thank ya', Lord."

Propping open her classroom door, Lydia stood beside it watching the students interact in the hallway, greeting every student personally as he entered the classroom, checking off each name as it was divulged to her, and attempting to notice something about each individual that would help her pin his name to him. When the last bell rang, the door was closed and Lydia took her place at the front of the room where, leaning on the edge of her desk, she could observe all the students' interactions for a few minutes to determine who were friends, and who were friendless. Reaching around to her desk, she retrieved a notebook on whose pages nothing was written, and then Lydia cleared her throat and called the room to attention.

"My name…" she began in a strong and firm voice that surprised even her, "…which I have written on the board, is Miss Marshall, and I am now going to organize this room by a seating arrangement."

There was a general uproar of disapproval, but Lydia ignored it, and looking down at her notebook as if the unwelcomed seating arrangement actually existed, she began to point to people and then to desks asking each person as she went around the room to uproot themselves from their present location and redeposit themselves in another, usually some good distance away from their best buddy.

One particularly shy girl had caught Lydia's attention before class when the girl went straight to the furthest corner of the classroom and sat there still and straight, talking to no one, and never looking around or up at anyone. This specific girl, whose name was Penny, Lydia placed in the front seat of the row nearest the door making it easy for the girl to slip in and out of class without having to walk in front of the other students, but where Lydia could call on her for answers and coax Penny to participate more each day in class activities. Lydia's hope was to win the confidence of this girl so that perhaps she would feel free to open up to Lydia about anything in her life that hindered her from being as functional as she wanted to be.

Most of the class had been satisfactorily repositioned as Lydia made her way slowly back up to the front of the room by way of the isle nearest the door. She looked up from her blank notebook just in time to see the impish (and obviously financially privileged) boy sitting in the desk behind unsuspecting Penny reaching up with his ink pen to somehow torment the painfully timid girl. Lydia walked up behind the unsuspecting boy and laid her hand on his shoulder. When he finally got the nerve to gaze up at her, she calmly, but intently, looked the boy in the eyes.

"Not on my watch…"

THE END

www.ingramcontent.com/pod-product-compliance
Lightning Source LLC
Chambersburg PA
CBHW051130020726
47501CB00005B/1428